# the
# helper

# the
# helper

M. M. DEWIL

BLACK
STONE
PUBLISHING

Copyright © 2024 by Incognito Productions
Published in 2024 by Blackstone Publishing
Cover and book design by Linley A. Delucchi

All rights reserved. This book or any portion
thereof may not be reproduced or used in any manner
whatsoever without the express written permission
of the publisher except for the use of brief quotations
in a book review.

The characters and events in this book are fictitious.
Any similarity to real persons, living or dead, is coincidental
and not intended by the author.

Originally published in hardcover by Blackstone Publishing in 2024

First paperback edition: 2024
ISBN 979-8-8746-7610-0
Fiction / Thrillers / Suspense

Version 1

Blackstone Publishing
31 Mistletoe Rd.
Ashland, OR 97520

www.BlackstonePublishing.com

*For Madhurika*

I don't look like the kind of person who could kill someone.

If you had asked me before it happened, I would've said the same thing . . . I'm not that kind of a person.

But then something happened.

And I did.

I killed someone.

# PART I

*Tout comprendre c'est tout pardonner.*
To understand all is to forgive all.
—French proverb

# one

I see him walk into the library and brace myself. It's instinctive. I know he'll smell and shout and the veins in his face will bulge, and Noreen will slip into the break room, and I will be left alone to deal with him.

Is there no one to help him, calm his rage? Does he live alone? I picture him in his apartment, shouting at his microwave, his reheated dinner, his suffering.

I notice the afternoon sun has found a crack between the buildings, through the window near the high ceiling of the library reception area, and now falls on the yellow flowers I brought in yesterday. The sun gives the day-old daisies life, but it's a hard light, not soft like a poem. Nothing is soft like the poems I read.

*Liberals! Cocksuckers! That's all it was, girlie boys! Shit on them! Shit!*

He's shouting as he slams the book on the counter. The shaft of light catches the drops of spittle flying from his mouth. His madness twinkles in the sun.

I can't go on like this, I know. It's not just Mad Manny or the rest of the freak show that uses the library for the bathroom and the free internet. The shield between me and the horror of my own possible homelessness is too thin, too feeble. I hear it creak from the heavy load of suffering above me. Will it crack? Will it all come crashing down on me? This constant tension has worn away my fortitude. I know, soon enough, something is going to break.

I push this thought aside. Like an exercise routine: *One and two and push away and three and four and push away.* It's tiring, like it should be. These thought exercises keep me lean and fit. I need to be the healthy Mary Williams, not the weak and soft one.

Mad Manny is mumbling to himself in the YA aisle. Mrs. Wygil is at the counter now. She's old. She once told me she's been coming to the library once a week for the last twenty years. The pile of books in front of her tell the story of a life still being lived:

*Breads, Cakes and Pastries*, by Beth Rose.

*Absent in the Spring*, by Agatha Christie.

*Ashtanga Yoga for Seniors*, by Ananda Sharma.

My day will be filled with library people like this: those that come in, and those I work with, like Noreen, who does less than everybody else, eating too much, hankering for someone to love her. She's still young, still believes a man can come and make all her problems go away. What she doesn't yet know is that a man can come and make all her *happiness* go away. And there's Ethel, the janitor, silent, like she once witnessed a murder and the killer threatened to come for her next if she ever said another word. Dean used to work here too. He seemed to be happy for some unknown reason. He would refile the books and smile and be kind to Ethel and ask me about my daughter. But he was retrenched, as were five others. It was almost me, gone . . . into unemployment, the shield between me and poverty shattering with the heavy weight of failure. Thank God it wasn't me. And so we went from nine to three, just like that. I had to take a pay cut and now work twice as hard . . . but thank God it wasn't me.

And then there are the patrons who come and go, and the regulars like Mad Manny and Mrs. Wygil and the young Asian boy who comes straight from school and never leaves the library until it closes. He's a nose-in-a-book boy. He even walks with his head down, as if he's reading an imaginary book on the floor that moves with him at each step. And Susan, the talker. So many words fall out of her small mouth. Like a broken tap, the words keep pouring out. The words have no value, no weight, no real meaning, and they keep coming until eventually even a polite listener, like me, starts to gaze at her and her tumbling flow of words and wonder how she cannot know that this is not a conversation or a chat or a catch-up but simply an assault on the potential peace of any given moment.

Eventually, Susan will see this, that she's gone too far, again, and now the tumbling words of a life unlived become the tumbling words of apology: *Listen to me going on again—you know me, once I get chatting, me and my chat, chat, chat . . . You're such a good listener . . . Surprised you don't run the other way when you see me coming. Never know when to keep quiet; my mom always used to say that.* "Little Miss Chatterbox," she said, "I should have got you a sister. Little Miss Chatterbox needs a sister." She said I should talk to the mirror, ha ha ha ha.

But some days are slow—no Susan, no Mad Manny. Some days are quiet, like it suddenly is now; the library gone still, a sliver carved out of the dull mania of life. The afternoon rays of sunlight have caught some dust. The particles rise and dip, like lazy ballerinas in a warm, floating sun-world.

It's a moment, a rare moment in a world of noise and ambition. These moments are like thin, delicate strands that could lead to something, something like happiness, but I know they're tenuous. I can't just tug on them. I have to be gentle, and the universe has to cooperate. Noreen can't just walk up behind me and ask me to cover for her while she goes to get a doughnut. A police car can't blast past with its obnoxious sirens. Sometimes, I can slowly melt into a moment like this, with the sun and the dancing dust and the hope of another world far from this one. Moments like this remind me of Hafiz, the Sufi poet.

One day, I saw a young man sitting at a desk in the far corner, reading. I was drawn to him. I kept looking at him for some reason I couldn't articulate. And then he looked up from his book straight at me. I saw he had tears in his eyes, but he was smiling. He looked so happy, and then Ethel was there, at my knees, trying to get to the plastic trash can under my desk. The mood broke; the delicate thread snapped. I didn't see him leave, but when it was time to close up, I saw the book was still on the table where he had sat. I went over. The book was *The Gift: Poems by Hafiz*.

It was open to a poem:

> *Your separation from God has ripened.*
> *Now fall like a golden fruit*
> *Into my hand.*

I flipped to another page and read some more:

> *What*
> *Do sad people have in*
> *Common?*
>
> *It seems*
> *They have all built a shrine*
> *To the past*

*And often go there
And do a strange wail and
Worship.*

*What is the beginning of
Happiness?*

*It is to stop being
So religious*

*Like*

*That.*

    I thought of the wet eyes of the young man, and unexpectedly, I felt my own eyes well up. Something within me opened up, for a moment.

    I have read every poem written by Hafiz since then. He became my confidant, my lover, my lifeline. I knew he was a gift, sent by providence. It was an acknowledgment of the beauty in the broken, a beauty no greater and no smaller than the beauty of the whole. On rare days, I give myself the luxury of imagining that Hafiz and I meet one day and he instantly understands everything about me, and in our mutual surrender, we shine a light bright enough to illuminate the world, banishing the darkness of fear forever. I need to do this because there are many more days not like that, days like yesterday, when I had to clean up vomit in the sci-fi/fantasy aisle.

# two

My daughter is two moves from mate. Although I'm not a very good player myself, I've watched enough games to know that she's got him—two moves and it's over. If she wins, she gets to compete in the East Coast Junior Tournament. She would like nothing more—she loves chess. If she wins this game, I'm going to have to find the money to get us to New York, for a hotel, for food. She's playing against an older boy; he's thirteen. She's seen the opening. He's made a mistake. It's the game right here, and he knows it. Then the boy looks at her; his lips part, and he smiles. Emma looks confused, clearly wondering, *Why is the boy smiling at me?* I don't like it the instant I see it. I know this look. He's manipulating her, and Em has no idea; she likes that the handsome but angry-looking boy is smiling at her.

*You're pretty,* he tells her.

Em looks stunned. I'm furious. So brazen. I want to get up from my seat in the back row of the gymnasium. I want to get up there and rip out his throat. Em is blushing, and the boy looks down like he's too shy to look at her. My blood boils.

Em loses.

The boy walks past us later and snorts in contempt at what

an easy play she was. Em is confused and upset. I say nothing about the boy.

*Next time, Em.*

We take the bus home in silence. There's a woman sitting in front of me. I see a small insect crawling in the swirl of gray hair on the back of her head.

# three

My friend Cyril has invited me to watch his theater group, *the Try-Hards*. It's their end-of-season performance. There are nine people in the audience, but everyone onstage seems to be having fun. I envy the thin man with a mustache, their lead actor. He really brings it as the enraged salesman from whom no one will buy toilet brushes.

*Three for the price of one! No? God dammit, where are you going to get a deal like that? No? What? Are you crazy? Okay, okay, five, five goddamn toilet brushes for the price of one!*

His eyes bulge in disbelief.

*No?! Have you lost your mind? I said five! What the hell is wrong with everyone?*

I want to do this. I want to scream, from my soul. I want to be naked up there and scream, let it all out like the thin man with the mustache is doing. He's giving everything he has for two polite chuckles. He doesn't care. I want to not care. To hell with what everyone thinks. But I can't. I'm scared, so I sit with the eight others and watch. Cyril is not very good. When he says his lines, I'm desperate for him to be convincing, but my eyes drift.

For the finale, there is a great confrontation, and the thin man with the mustache stabs a plump girl in the heart. The fake-blood pouch tears, and the red liquid spreads over her blouse. It actually looks quite convincing.

*Thank you, Jacksonville,* he says with a dramatic bow.

I'm nervous on the drive home with Cyril. What do I say? It seems he's not doing his part—he's not being brave, onstage and maybe in life too. He never commits to asking me out, always waiting for me to give the indication that it's okay to ask. He's been on and off with me for a year now, not friend, not boyfriend, not brave. But I smile and tell him it was very good. I play my unbrave part for him. We park outside my apartment complex. He's kissing me; it's uncomfortable. Outside, I see someone is walking his dog under the streetlight. The dog stops and does its business. The man bends over and picks up the poop with his little doggy bag.

Cyril has a noticeable erection that I'm desperate not to look at. The man with his dog walks past our car. His green bag of dog shit sways from his hand, *swish, swish,* across his sweatpants.

# four

The next morning Em is hunched over and laughing so hard Rice Krispies are shooting out of her mouth. She's trying to tell me what has set her off like this. *It's a video of a woman in very high heels and . . .* Something, something. Em can't get the rest out without breaking down in hysterics each time she tries to explain it. She hands the phone to me. I watch a woman slip in her heels and then take several steps, trying to stop herself falling. Somehow, ridiculously, she manages to not fall over, but the momentum forces her to take wider and wider steps to remain upright. It's over the top and hilarious. It's like me trying to win at life. I start laughing too. We laugh for minutes. My stomach hurts.

Later, we walk to the bus stop. She waves goodbye and then starts to mimic the wide-stepping high-heeled woman we just watched. She starts laughing again as she enters the bus.

Who is she? This ray of light. Without her, this world would have no meaning.

Watching her head off to school, I have to catch myself, have to hold back the flow of fear and pity that I feel for myself from spilling out onto her. She is not me. She is strong and funny and capable of going on to lead a fulfilled life.

But is that true; do I really believe that? Have my broken marriage and my near poverty ruined things for her? Is she destined to carry those unhealthy wounds through her own life, destined to falter at crucial times, lacking the inherent confidence of those with wealthy and married parents? Is she doomed?

She's not doomed, but her position is precarious. Her adolescence, the start of her life as a woman, is a crucial time; if there's a knock now, a storm too strong, she could grow askew. *Push away and one and two and push away and three and four.* But she has me, and I know there is little I wouldn't do to protect her. It's the only kind of ferocity I have. It's primal. It's there to ensure her healthy growth. The thought of her in the world alone at this tender age, without me . . . it's unbearable. But thankfully, she does have me.

And I have her . . . the one thing that makes my life bearable, her crooked smile my respite from a harsh world. We're a team, she and I, giggling at the baby and dog videos on YouTube, singing together the *Growing Pains* theme song:

> *As long as we got each other,*
> *we got the world spinnin' right in our hands.*
> *Baby, you and me,*
> *we gotta be*
> *the luckiest dreamers who never quit dreamin'.*

But I don't burden her with the weight of how much she means to me. She needs the space to grow. She needn't see the gardener in the background, tilling the soil, getting rid of the bugs, quietly building shelters for the squalls to come.

Alone now. Em has gone to school, and I have twenty minutes before my bus. The pile of bills on the kitchen table considers me. They have no malice. They are just what they are: requests for payment for services rendered. But they feel merciless, bringing nothing but anxiety. I haven't the strength to open them. Some of them have been there for months. I've tried to not even look at them. I know just by a glance—the envelope they are in, the typeface of the address—which bills they are. In spite of this great identification skill, however, I still have no money to pay for them.

They sit there. I sit there. Sometimes it feels like only one of us can survive. I force myself to look at the pile. It's just paper and ink, I say to myself. But I know it's also humiliation.

# five

I'm standing inside Mr. Stewart's office at the library, but it feels like I'm floating in another world. It seems so extreme and heightened and frankly unbelievable. I feel light, not as if I'm going to fall over but as if I might blow away. I have no connection to the ground anymore, no weight to hold me down. It's a peculiar, unnerving sensation, one I haven't felt before. This must be what it's like in a novel. This isn't the hero's triumph, though. No, this is the other part, the opposite of that. This is where everything goes wrong, where the worst thing happens and the reader gasps. This is the part where I'm standing opposite Mr. Stewart after he's told me that the library has to do more cutbacks and they have to let me go. That they can only afford to keep one person, and they've decided to keep Noreen. I hear his words, but they don't make sense. Then I see his face, the look of pity, and only then do I realize what this means. It means it's real. The words he's saying are real.

My fear earlier was a harbinger. It knew this day would come.

He sees the realization grow over my face, the horror sink

into my bones. He looks at me helplessly, emasculated by the reality that he has no agency in the destiny of my life.

———

The bus ride home from work is not like the bus ride I took to work. Although it's the same bus and it's the same route, the person who went into work was a different person from the person going home. The ride into work was for someone who had been able to survive the world, not in any noteworthy way, but survive nonetheless, and raise a daughter who might have a better life than her own.

The ride back is a journey for someone else. This is for a person who will surely not survive, who will be homeless, a person whose mind has already reminded her of that place under the bridge, next to the trees, where the other homeless people live. She has noticed it would not be such a bad place if that nightmare ever came true and she too needed a place on the streets. This is the ride of a person whose ex-husband will certainly now try to get custody of her child. This is the ride of a person who can see now that Hafiz, the great Sufi poet, knew nothing and was just an eccentric old fool with the cushioning of wealth that enabled him to talk of a dancing and playful God.

———

I sit at the kitchen table. It's quiet and I wonder when I'm going to cry. Am I still in shock? I know what he said: *We can only afford to keep Noreen.* Noreen? Is this a joke? She doesn't even want to do the job. *I'm sorry* and then that look. I stare into the middle distance. My brain is racing to catch up. The consequences of this are so devastating and so far reaching, affecting so many aspects of my life, that I struggle to assimilate it all.

And then I think of Em. And then the tears come.

I'm happy I'm alone because nobody should have to see this. The snot, the howling. I'm on the floor, rocking and wailing.

*We wish you the best for the future.*

I can't move. I don't want to move. Maybe if I just stay here on the kitchen floor with the broken washing machine and the bulk cereal packs, maybe it won't be real. Is it possible that this isn't truly happening? I replay the morning, going into the library, happy to see my new, English edition of the Bhagavad Gita has arrived. The dialogue on the battlefield, the warrior Arjuna reluctant to fight, and Krishna explaining that raising his bow is the kindest thing he can do. I remember the book in my hand, the cover with the disconsolate Arjuna, head in his hands, bow on the ground. I remember Mr. Stewart beside me, asking if he might have a quick word; I remember the tightening in my chest. It wasn't a dream. It happened. I cry again, but the tears lack their former ferocity.

Will we survive? I think of Em; what I would do for her. I remember the story of a young mother who held up her car to save her child trapped underneath. I researched the story. They even have a term for it: *hysterical strength*—a show of extreme strength, beyond what is seen as normal, usually in life-and-death situations. Common examples include mothers lifting cars to rescue their children. Am I hysterical? Will I have that strength? Or is that, too, something that I don't have in this life?

I know that extreme fear . . . how consuming it can be, how you are willing to do anything, almost anything, to get rid of it. Particularly to save the ones we love. Remember the man who cut off his arm when it was trapped under a boulder? I read his book. He didn't seem hysterical, though. It was the opposite; he seemed calm and rational, like a man.

*You're being hysterical.*

My husband jabbed at me like a short-bladed knife into my gut.

*Calm down.*

Stab. As we stood in the waiting room of the hospital.

*What's wrong with you?*

Stab.

*You're unstable.*

Stab.

David could have helped; he could have told me that it was going to be okay, that the doctors knew what they were doing. He could have reassured me that it was not life threatening. But he didn't. He looked at me with scorn, and I wondered about this man I had married—where was his care while our daughter lay in intensive care with meningitis? But I held on to my strength then, and Em recovered and grew strong, unlike my marriage, which withered and died.

Em will be home soon. *Push away and one and two and push away and three and four.*

I grasp inside for a memory of Strong Mary, the Mary who told the bully teasing her friend Mato that what he was saying about him was not true. That Mato had as much right to be in this country as he did. *His ancestors were here long before the white people arrived.* I see again the determination in my little face. The little girl who could never abide cruelty.

What happened?

David happened. Slowly but surely I let him steal the strong, independent parts from me until I was compliant and meek, just how he liked it. A robbery in broad daylight.

Why did I become weak when I had once been strong?

Fear?

I see it like a black blob of a man sitting on the old kitchen chair, looking at me, leering at me, like that boy at the chess game. He's going to do what he wants with me; he's going to—
*No, stop this.*

I shake my head slowly, and it takes a while before I get up and move around the small apartment. He's still there, this anti-Hafiz, this killer of joy, this black blob-shaped fearmonger. He follows me as I go to the bathroom. I think this is how it will end. The black blob will grow big. He will take over everything.

If I'm to survive, I have to push past him, use my hands to shove aside the formless black shame that will block every single step forward. He wants me on my knees; he wants me hunched in the fetal position so he can slowly slide over me and suffocate me, suck out any hope, make me finally surrender to my fate as a worthless person.

I suddenly, urgently want my father. I want him to wrap me in his arms and tell me everything is going to be okay. But he's gone. As is my mother. And there is no sibling. Only a deaf uncle in Texas.

There was once David. I loved his surety. He said, *I've got this. I'll take care of it.* And he did.

---

But then I remember David scolding me. When things turned bad for him, he would rage, slamming his fist into the wall, his lips curled in contempt. And then his discontent, his rage, turned to me.

*Don't be pathetic.*
Now it's just me.
And Em.
There is no lifeline.

# six

Em is surprised to see me at the bus stop. I tell her that I got laid off but not to worry: I have a new job already lined up. She looks at me, a penetrating stare older than her twelve years of age. Does she know that I am worthless too? Does she know that I'm lying? *Push away and one and two.*

―――

*Oh, yes, um, yes, she should be able to attend.*

*It's a concussion, and the doctors are pretty sure he'll be out for some weeks. They're recommending he doesn't tax his brain too much.*

*I'm sorry to hear that.*

*So can we confirm Emma?*

*Um, yes, yes.*

*Great. The entrance fee is four hundred fifty dollars. They're asking that we all book at the Hyatt. There's a discount for the out-of-state teams. So we are all pitching in together on that. I hope it's okay. I'll send you the link. Please tell Emma we look forward to seeing her there.*

*Um, okay, yes, thank you.*

I hang up. Four hundred fifty dollars. The Hyatt.
*What?* Em is looking at me.
*Rick Stevens got a concussion—he can't play. You're the next alternate.*
Em's eyes widen, and her mouth starts to climb into a big smile. But then she adds: *Dad can pay. I'll ask him, don't worry.*
She smiles. Not the big smile. The sad smile. The sad smile that makes the black blob grow.
She doesn't know the mess I made with the divorce, my naivete, how easily David manipulated me. She doesn't know about the "joint debt" he tricked me with, how much control he has over child support, the conditions of my living arrangement with Em. He played me like a fool, and now almost every cent he gives me for Em's care is seen as his act of charity and not a legal right.
Yes, David will pay. And later Weak Mary will pay too.

———

I wake at 2:23 a.m. and flip open the old Dell. The numbers row doesn't work properly. I have to copy and paste from previous numbers I stored in a Word file. I start looking for jobs, any job. This is not a joke. I need the money. The shame is morphing into urgency. Craigslist. Indeed. JobsRUs. Any job, any website.
Who will hire a middle-aged librarian with no discernible skills? *Push away and three and four.*
Glassdoor. ZipRecruiter. HelpWanted.
*Who wants a loser? Everyone wants winners. Push away and three and four.*
SimplyHired. CoolWorks. FlexJobs. CareersUnlimited. JobsJobsJobs.
I keep going.
Is this mania? Is this my hysterical strength? My eyes hurt

from the blue glow of the too-bright screen. But I force them open and I keep going. From accounting to zoo hand, I go through hundreds and hundreds of jobs. I'm qualified for almost none of them, but anything with no experience necessary or on-the-job training, I apply for.

Name:
*Mary the Weak*

Address:
*Soon to be homeless*

Education:
*As unremarkable as my personality*

Additional information:
*Generally insecure and—*
Push away and one and two and
Send *swoosh*
Send *swoosh*
Send *swoosh*
And immediately:
*Ping*
*Ping*

A message that you sent could not be delivered to one or more of its recipients. This is a permanent error. The following address(es) failed:

devries@jobsjobsjobs.com
jones34@coolworks.com
job223@flexjobs.com

And twenty-one more like this. Still, I push on.

And then I can't type another letter. Exhaustion crashes into me like a head-on truck. I put my head down on the keyboard . . .

*Sssrrrrrggggggggggggggggggggggggggggggggggggggggggggggggggggggggggggggggggggg* beep, beep, beep

I jolt up. I fill out nine more job applications for anything with even a remote chance. And then I go to bed, careful not to wake Em, whose bed is in the same room, and fall asleep instantly.

---

Em wakes me an hour and fifteen minutes later. It's morning. *Mom, Mom, are you okay?*

Fear overwhelms me instantly. I know I can't hold up the shield anymore; the weight on top of it is too great. I can't protect her or myself from it crashing down on us both. Who could? No one could survive this. But I don't say that. Instead, I try to smile and hope the smile is not tinged with mania.

*We need more bread. I used the crusts.*

She's dressed, backpack over her shoulder and ready to go.

*I'll go by myself. See you later.*

She leans in and gives me a kiss.

I want to say something, but I can't. The truth is too much, and she won't fall for an unthought-out lie. I hear the door close behind her. I lie there staring up at the ceiling. How do I do this? Where is the energy to get out of bed, stand up, and be a person in the world? How do I face what is my life? How do people do this? I will my abdominal muscles to contract, pull my torso up, get out of bed.

I open Gmail. There are twenty-three new emails. Eighteen are failed delivery notifications, and the other five are junk mail.

It takes time, I tell myself. Something will come.

I look at the books I brought home from the library. The Bhagavad Gita, about the warrior Arjuna who didn't want to fight anymore. I don't want to fight anymore. I've never wanted to fight. Why does there have to be opposition to a happy, harmonious life? Do we not all want the same thing? No. We don't. I wanted to remain married. David didn't want to be married anymore. There is no common center. Is that God? My God? Your God? What I want may be in opposition to what you want, and then there is no harmony anymore. And so we fight. I don't want to fight. But I can't stop, not now. I have to fight . . . for Em. I put the book down. Who has time for Vedic texts and the enlightened poet Hafiz? You can't feed a hungry daughter philosophy.

I didn't come from wealth, but my parents taught me how to save and be responsible with money. However, they also taught me obedience. And after I met David and we got married, he said he could get better returns by investing my savings instead of just keeping the money in the bank. So I let him lead, and dealing with the money became his department. And then came the divorce, and I was told there was no money anymore. And now everything rests on my shoulders, and the weight is so very heavy.

The phone rings. It's shrill. I flinch and close my eyes. I have to fight every instinct to crawl under the bed and not come out until things are safe again. But if I do that, I know I will weaken with each hour, slowly succumb, the shield above me breaking, and Em and I will drown in the avalanche of bad things falling upon us.

I don't recognize the number. Maybe it's a response to one of the job applications? I answer. It's not. It's David's lawyer's assistant. She wants to set a time for a house inspection. Judge ordered. David is still trying to get custody of Em. Claims of

unfit living conditions. A sour memory bubbles up. David screaming at me. Why is he always screaming?
*You can't give her what she needs. You're unfit.*
I tell the woman to please email me. I give her more patience and politeness than I have. I need to do this. If I don't, I feel the dam will break. And then who knows what I will do.
*Unfit.* Will he get Em? Even if she doesn't want to go? I'm afraid of the answer.

# seven

Five hundred eighty-nine dollars and five cents.

This is the amount of money I have left on my three credit cards. I am $63,000 in debt. I am overdue on the rent. I have exceeded my last warning from the landlord. Rent is $500. That leaves $89 for food and utilities and bus fare and chess fees and everything else a person needs just to live in this world. I will make this work. I know I can. Deep down I know this is a lie. I know I have no way of knowing if I can or cannot do this. Deep down I know this is not in my hands.

*You can do it.*

*You can do it.*

How? I wonder in a moment of perfect clarity. How is this done? Are we at the miracle stage here? Without one we're bust. My mood darkens, frustration letting anger slip in through a back door: he did this—David, he did this.

His lawyers managed to convince the court that his debts were in fact joint debts, "*debts for equitable distribution*," his debts that I had to pay too. So in the end not only did I have nothing, but I had less. I owed.

David did this. David, who made me a signatory on his

business loans. David with his wealthy parents. David the Cruel, who destroyed Mary the Once Strong.

*Push away and three and four.* And then:

*Ping*

I instinctively know what this is. This is a reply to one of the job applications. I know it. It's 10:14 a.m., and someone has come in to work, read the incoming emails, and responded to my application. For the briefest of moments, I feel a surge of relief. Everything is going to be okay. I'll get another job, the shield will hold, and Em will grow up unscathed by the failings of her mother.

I try to hold this feeling, but I can't. It slips through my grasp like smoke. In its place comes something else. Dread. There are no openings for a middle-aged failure. *We regret to inform you that after due consideration we found you have no redeeming qualities and as such . . .*

One and two and push away.

I will myself to walk over to the old Dell on the kitchen table. I will myself to keep going. I have more fight in me.

I sit down, click the touch pad. Gmail is open, and there is a blue *1* in my inbox: b128c7397d59783f@reply.craigslist.org. *Re: Helper needed.*

I feel a tremor in my body. Craigslist doesn't normally send replies to unsuccessful applications. I click to open the email.

**Hi Mary, thx for responding. If you are still interested would you like to meet to discuss the details? Please call me when you can. Kindly, Eric**

I click on the link to the listing at the bottom of the email. I have no idea what job this is.

> Helper wanted. End-of-life caregiver. Start immediately, no previous experience required but must be committed and willing to go the extra mile.

I can do that. Immediately everything changes. Everything *is* going to be okay. My worry seems childish now, hysterical. I need to be more chill. Things happen; I can't be so easily devastated. My mind starts firing, hustling, planning, thinking, imagining what to do, what not to do, how this will play out, what kind of salary to expect— *Push away and three and four.* I breathe. Yes, this too, the flip side of the negative, must also stop. Exhale. I blink, trying to slow myself down.

> Dear Eric, thank you so much for your reply. I would be delighted to meet you to discuss the details of the job. Just let me know a date and time and I will be there.

I read my reply. Too desperate. I try again.

> Dear Eric, thank you for your reply. Please let me know when would be a good time to call. Best, Mary Williams.

I reread it. Suddenly I'm nervous again. What if he doesn't like my tone? The reality of how precarious my life is stares back at me again. I need this job more than anything else. I search through the tossing ocean of my mind for some kind of life raft, something to cling to, to stop me from being broken apart on the rocks of fear, hope, and dread.

> *Out*
> *Of a great need*
> *We are all holding hands*

> *And climbing.*
> *Not loving is a letting go.*
> *Listen,*
> *The terrain around here*
> *Is*
> *Far too*
> *Dangerous*
> *For*
> *That.*

Hafiz whispers in my ear.
I breathe. Inhale, exhale. Inhale, exhale.
I was once Mary the Strong. I can be again. I hit send: *Swish.*
Will it make it, this email, weighed down by the heavy weight of consequence? Will it stumble just before Eric's inbox? How many others have applied for this job? Others with experience, others without the shame and desperation that clings to me. How many others have— STOP!

I shout aloud to myself at the kitchen table. I can't take it anymore.

*Just stop it.*

Softer this time. I start to wash the dishes. I practice mental discipline. Control what you can control, let go of the rest. There is nothing tha— *Ping.*

A reply? That quickly?

**Free now 362-211-8989.**

My heart pounds. Now?
*Hello, is this Eric?*
*Yes, you must be Mary.*
*Yes, yes, I am.*

*Thank you for replying to my ad.*
*Oh, yes, of course, um . . .*
*So, I think we need to meet so I can explain what this entails.*
*Yes, of course, anytime.* Slow down, I tell myself.
*How about the Waffle House on the 441 at noon. Can you make that?*
*Yes, um, yes, I can.*
Does the bus go past the 441?
*I will wear a navy scarf.*
*Um, okay, I will see you then.*

I hang up. I look at my watch. It's 11:16 a.m. So help me God, I can't be late. The goal in front of me becomes crystal clear. All my focus goes into getting ready and finding a way to the Waffle House on the 441 before noon. I check the bus routes. The 27 leaves Main Street at 11:31 a.m. and gets to the corner of the 441 and Clyde Street at 12:03, plus a fifteen-minute walk to the Waffle House. Eighteen minutes late. That won't work. Uber? I can't afford an Uber. I check. Twenty-three dollars. I can take the bus back. It's only a twenty-minute drive. It gives me time to get dressed and eat. I need food in my stomach to settle my nerves. Eating is the last thing I want to do, but I know I need to do it.

My mind is already spinning. I force myself to slow down. I'll take the Uber—I have no choice—and I will not think about the extraordinary extravagance. I'll eat, and then I'll get changed, and then I will go. The small manageable tasks give me purpose. I don't have to secure the job that keeps my daughter and me housed and fed. I just have to shower, then find something to wear, then order the Uber, then go inside and find the man in the navy scarf.

*You've got this, Mary.*

# eight

The Uber driver's name is Deshaun. A little green tree hanging from his rearview mirror strains to mask the heavy odor of stale sweat in the car. He doesn't talk, thankfully, but he is playing rap music. I want to ask him to turn it down, but I can't. No matter how polite I am, he might take offense, and I'd have to sit in the resulting tension for the rest of the trip.

> *This is a Rollie, not a stopwatch, shit don't ever stop.*
> *This is the flow that got the block hot.*

Is that a big problem in the rap world? People confusing Rolex watches for stopwatches? I notice a sign hanging over the passenger-seat headrest: *Hey, you back there, tips appreciated, just sayin'*. I can barely afford this ride. How much am I expected to tip? I google as we drive. According to a study, 68 percent of people don't tip on Uber rides. I'm relieved and disappointed at the same time. What happened to us? But then I know the answer: Living is expensive. Our debts grew. We started to struggle in places our parents hadn't. And that changed us, changed how we dealt with the world. But I don't want to be like that.

I give him two dollars when he drops me off, although I don't make eye contact, afraid it won't be enough.

I stand outside the Waffle House. I'm here at nine minutes before noon. I walk inside, grateful for a few moments to get composed. I see the blue scarf immediately as I walk in.

He stands, makes eye contact, and beckons for me to come over. I'm taken aback. I thought I'd have a little time. I wanted to go to the bathroom, check my makeup. I want to do some breathing, rehearse some answers. But here he is, pale and thin. He's wearing a baby-blue windbreaker that seems too much for this warm weather. His hair is neat and recently cut. He smiles, but it's a strain, I can see.

*Thank you for coming.*

I try to say something in reply, but the words get stuck in my throat. I've rushed into this out of desperation, and I have no idea what I'm doing. I'm stumbling over my words. He doesn't seem to mind. He looks down like he's suddenly very tired.

*Forgive me if I get right to it, but you see, this is not really me interviewing you. It's really* . . . He takes a breath. *It's a matter of you—if you are prepared to help me with my* . . . *situation. If you are* . . . *you have the job.*

I cannot say how grateful I am to hear these words. I've already confirmed in my mind that I'm willing to do just about anything—clean toilets, wipe up vomit, whatever. At least for now, until I manage to save more money, I will do pretty near anything. Immediately any pressure about what will happen in the next minutes disappears, like it was never there in the first place. I feel light and tremendously relieved.

*To be honest, I really need the work, so I'm sure I'll be able to help.*

He starts talking. He tells me what he would like me to do to help him. As he does, my brain is assimilating the words and the meaning, and I try to comprehend and make sense of them. But another part of me, a deeper part, does not accept his words. They are too bizarre; what he's saying has no reference in the rational world. This other part of me leaves the Waffle House; this part of me finds itself in a lush forest or a green sea or an emerald cloud, something full and encompassing, where I drift alone. I want to leave behind the words that he is saying. I want to ignore their obvious meaning. I want to imagine another meaning.

But his words keep pulling me back from the warm sun.

*I know this is not what you were expecting to hear.*

*Go higher, go higher, Mary*, I will myself. The warmth is my friend.

*This may seem like a drastic measure . . .*

But I'm getting colder.

I'm going backward and twirling back to the ground, away from the warmth.

*Please consider what I said, what state I must be in to ask this . . .*

Back through the green forest.

*I acknowledge this is shocking.*

Back to the Waffle House.

*I wouldn't ask this unless I was absolutely sure this was the only choice.*

Back to the booth, where this pale, neatly dressed man has just finished telling me the most audacious thing I've ever heard.

# nine

The moment Eric sees her, he feels she might just be the one. Something about the fear in her eyes. Eric knows that for someone to do what he needs them to do, there must be a level of desperation.

She doesn't know that nine other people have sat in that exact same seat over the last twelve days and Eric didn't feel confident enough about a single one of them to risk telling them what he really wanted from them.

But seeing her, seeing that fear and desperation, seeing her nervously stumble over her words, Eric knows he's going to risk it. He's going to tell her everything.

With the others, he wasn't sure. He let them talk, trying to gauge if they had it in them, if he could risk telling them what he really wanted them to do. But then they would do something, say something, that made him pull back. And ultimately, with every one of them, he would smile and say that he'd get back to them, which of course he never did.

But with Mary Williams, he doesn't know why he is so sure, but he decides to tell her. And Mary, he's sure, will agree to do it, if not immediately then very shortly afterward.

And so, when her water arrives and he sees the slight tremor in her hands, he tells her the job is hers if she wants it. He tells her he can see she is a kind person and that's all he's really looking for.

And then he tells her what the job entails.

# ten

Em has asked her father if he can pay for the chess tournament and hotel in New York. He said yes, of course.
*Even better, I'll take you.*
Em is torn. She loves chess, but she doesn't want to go with her father. She can tolerate going with him, but she wants me to go, and she knows I want to go too. I love watching her stare at the pieces, forming a plan of attack, a buttress of defense. It's the most life-affirming thing I've ever witnessed. To observe this young girl, that young mind turning over, is to believe and have hope. But we both know there is no way that David is not going. There's no way he will back down, be reasonable, conciliatory. There is no way she can tell him that he can pay but she wants to go with me. I reassure her that it will be fun.
*Go! New York! You'll kick butt.*
She smiles. In spite of the enormous trauma her divorced parents have caused to her fragile growth, still, she smiles. She loves to compete. She's good at it. Her fight gives me the power to smash through walls on her behalf.
*Go; bring home the gold. Take no prisoners.*
Em disappears into the bedroom. I stare out the window.

I wake up at two in the morning staring at the ceiling. I knew this would happen. I knew my mind wouldn't let it go, not something as outrageous as what that man told me. It's not possible. Never in a million years would I do something like that. It would be easy to just dismiss it, but there's a single element to the story that I know will gnaw at me until I die. It's a single cancerous cell that will eventually infect every other healthy cell I have. It's the contaminant.

It's $100,000.

One one and five zeros.

Like a code that unlocks the safe that holds all the things I so desperately need. What those numbers could mean, to me, to Em. The minute he told me that number, I could feel my mind responding immediately, as if to an expert lover who has your full attention with just one kiss. I knew my mind would not rest. I knew even as I politely, although clearly, told Eric Smith that I would not be able to do what he was asking and that I wished him well and left . . . I knew that this was not over. I knew I would have to deal with it. I would have to deal with a little seed that was starting to grow in the back of my mind.

One hundred thousand dollars.

I'm sure that many people think that's not such a large sum of money. I'm sure there are many who would judge me for thinking that that amount of money would really change my life. I understand that. There was a time, before David's divorce lawyers, before the *"joint debt,"* before the slow descent toward poverty, when I would have thought that too.

*Money can't buy happiness,* I remember once telling Em. We had gone to a birthday party for one of her school friends. *She's rich,* Emma had told me. I remember walking into the house and seeing the high ceilings, the tasteful art, the bespoke hors d'oeuvres, the personalized cupcakes, *Emma* written in pink frosting. And still thinking we had enough, Em and I. We didn't need all these material things to be happy. The pursuit of money is for those unable to enjoy the inherent beauty of life. Money might have gotten that girl a diamond locket from her mom, but it can't buy happiness. Those are separate things, a diamond locket and happiness.

Little did I know.

You can't feed a hungry person philosophy.

I blink in the dark. I hear Em breathing in her bed against the wall on the other side of the room.

One hundred thousand dollars.

Me and Emma. Emma and me. The dream team. Inseparable. But now with the means to do all the things we wanted.

But it's clear to me that I'll never be able to do what the man asked. It's just not in the realm of possibility. However, what's not clear is how I am going to get my mind under some kind of control.

I practice positive thinking to still the swirling in my head:

*I will receive several replies to my applications tomorrow.*

*I will interview with a handful of places and start work at my new job before the end of the month.*

*Yes, it won't be $100,000, but it will be enough. And Em and I will continue to move through this world with kindness and hope.*

I lie there. The room, the world, is silent and dark.

Seconds pass.

Stillness.

I blink.

More seconds pass.

David will take Em if I have no money.

*No.*

*Be still.*
*Breathe.*
*Exhale.*

---

Em is waking me up again. She's dressed and on her way to school.
*Hey, lazy log, what's going on? See you when I get back.*
*No, I'm up. Sorry, I don't know what's gotten into me.*
I swing my feet over the bed quickly, a little too quickly. I'm disoriented as I get to my feet and fumble for my robe. Em laughs. Is there a hint of concern in there? Is my eagerness to act normal telling?
*Come, let me make you breakfast. What do you want to—*
*It's eight eleven, Mom. You're an hour off. I got to go. See ya—I'm out of here.*
I stand there, trying to hide my bewilderment. She's waving, smiling. She closes the door behind her, and then she's gone.
I'm alone. The apartment is suddenly very still. Moments click by, and then, from some dark recess in my mind, I hear a voice whisper: *One hundred thousand dollars.*

# eleven

*I have tinnitus. It's a ringing in the ear. I have a very severe case. I don't think I've had more than an hour of uninterrupted sleep in the last ten years. The doctors think a cyst might be pinching an auditory nerve, but to this day they have been unable to find anything conclusive.*

Eric sees her processing this. He sees her thinking that this is manageable for her, that she could help a person with tinnitus.

*That sounds terrible.*

*It's constant. It's like a mixture between a ring and a hum. I've been on every allopathic drug available. I've tried every alternative treatment too, acupuncture, fasting, Ayurveda. Nothing has worked. The pain drugs helped with the sleep at first. They were so strong they just knocked me out, and I could sleep. But slowly my body got accustomed to the dose and the efficacy wore off. The sound remains the same and as consistent as ever.*

Eric pauses, squeezes his eyes shut, and rubs the side of his head. He takes his time.

*It's caused a lot of stress . . .* He trails off, to give her a moment, then continues.

*It was explained to me by one of the many doctors I've seen over the years that it's like the auditory nerve connected to my brain has begun to fray, and the brain tries to compensate for the loss of hearing by turning up the internal volume. It's maddening. Every little thing is too loud. Just the sound of your nail gently rubbing against the linoleum counter is nearly impossible to handle.*

Mary looks down at her nail.

*Or the sound of that small piece of paper caught in the end of the air conditioner above the door makes me want to scream. This is the first time I've been out in months. I wanted to ask the candidates for the job to come and interview in my apartment, but I'm sure that I would've made people uncomfortable. So I had to come out. The truth is, Mary, there is no cure for this. It's been around for centuries. There's been no cure for hundreds of years, and the doctors have no hope of one coming anytime soon.*

He lets that hang in the air for a dramatic moment.

*My condition is getting worse. I barely leave the house. I'm like a prisoner, and even in my tinnitus-proofed home, even without much external noise, the internal volume is increasing.*

He pauses again.

*Sleep deprivation is the kind of torture that people use when they're trying to break down someone's mind. I used to swim. I used to play piano. I used to laugh. I've lost over seventy pounds in the last five years from the stress of the noise.*

He looks at her, holds the look, wants her to see him.

*I need help. I can't go on like this. I just can't.*

He can see she's moved; this is clearly a woman with her own pain, able to identify quickly with the pain of others, an empath. This is good.

*You need to tell her the other part,* the little voice whispers to him. *Tell her.*

# twelve

I check my inbox. Five new emails. Four of them are junk mail; one is a reply to a job. I open it quickly, afraid it will go away if I don't.

Congratulations! Your application has been approved!

Thank God. Thank God. Thank God. I don't know what the job is and I don't care. But I'm taking it. It's from Text Co. I only have a dim recollection of what they do. I click on the URL.

Your opportunity to work as a chat operator and earn an average of 300 USD weekly is only minutes away! Reclaim your freedom today and start working whenever you please! Confirm your application details now.

Three hundred USD a week times four equals twelve hundred USD, minus tax equals under a thousand dollars.
My heart sinks again to its familiar place of disappointment.

As a chat operator, you will be answering casual messages on a fantasy-based adult chat network. You have to be able to talk to customers about all kinds of topics. You will be assigned different roles, depending on what your customer wants. Some of our clients just want to talk to someone about everyday life. Small talk about things like work, culture, weather, relationships. Your identity will not be known by customers.

A fantasy-based adult chat network? I read it again. And then further . . .

- Decide when, where, and how much you want to work
- No qualifications necessary
- 100% anonymous
- Chat only, no calling or video

Chat only, no calling or video. This is clearly some kind of online sex thing, a niche that somehow the flood of porn has not fully saturated yet. Can I do this, send suggestive messages to anonymous men? I'm sure this is men, in suits and ties, in offices and conference calls and business trips.

I refresh my Gmail. Nothing.

I look at the pile of unopened mail on the table next to me. It's like a standoff. They're not moving, and I'm not opening them, each of us refusing to budge. But I know they always win. They will sit there forever. I will eventually break.

I decide I have to face this. I reach over, take the one I know I cannot ignore any longer, and rip it open. The untidiness of the torn edge of the envelope makes me uncomfortable. Is there not a better way to do this? Then I remember letter openers, the knives they use in those Agatha Christie novels to kill the lady of the manor.

Unable to delay any longer, I pull out the folded letter. It's an official three-day notice to pay rent or quit. I look at the date on the letter: the twelfth, two weeks ago. I wonder if this is it. Will the landlord really ask us to leave? Put us on the street? I received one of these before. He didn't kick us out, but I did pay him three weeks later. I go back to the Text Co. site. Three hundred dollars a week. I click on the testimonials.

> By working as a chat operator, you can freely schedule your day. This is huge, especially for me, who became a father last year. It meant I could work during the afternoon when my son is sleeping and spend the extra money on my living expenses, which is very helpful.

This is from Steven. There's a photo. *Is that you, Steven?* Or is this just some picture from the web? I should do a retro search for this photo. Is that the term? This is so clearly a sex chatting thing, and they're going out of their way to pretend it's not.

A vein of insecurity throbs up within me.

*What if their clients don't want to chat with me?*

I'm sad at how pathetic that sounds. The confirm button blinks back at me on their website.

# thirteen

*How exactly do you want me to help?* she asks.

*What I'm about to tell you is going to sound extreme, but please hear me out,* he says.

*Two years ago, I tried to take my own life. I took a lot of pills that I thought would be enough to end all my suffering. My boyfriend found me, I was rushed to the hospital, and my stomach was pumped. I survived, but my stomach lining and liver suffered permanent damage. On top of the tinnitus, I now have near-permanent abdominal pain and a compromised immune system. I also get fluid retention in my legs, which makes it harder for me to sleep.*

He pauses. Here comes the difficult part.

*I cannot go on like this anymore, so I have bought a gun to kill myself.*

Her eyes widen, but Eric can see that she's still there, still invested in helping in some way.

*Recently my mother was diagnosed with acute diabetes. Her treatment is critical and very expensive. She has no money. I've been caring for her and paying her bills for the last eleven months. If I kill myself, my life insurance won't pay out.*

# fourteen

Sex work? That's what this is. Sure, there's no real sex involved, but it would be hard to fool myself that it's not sex work. Could I do that? I wonder. If I could do that, why not the other thing the sickly man asked me to do at the Waffle House? I remember the daunting realization of what he was asking. At first, the disbelief came. Was he really asking me to shoot him? I remember looking around—for what, I wasn't sure. Maybe I was afraid someone had heard him. Maybe I was checking if I was indeed back from the green forest, was indeed in the real world, with a man sitting opposite me in a booth at the Waffle House asking if I would please shoot him in the head so that he could end this life of suffering and ensure that his mother received the insurance money to continue her chronic diabetes treatment.

This is what happens in the novels I read.

How did I find myself in a novel? How did I find myself sitting opposite a man asking me to shoot him in the head for $100,000?

I wonder if he will be able to find someone who will do that. There must be people out there who would do this for him.

My chest tightens in a squeeze of panic. Maybe this is my final chance to get out of the suffocation of poverty. Maybe I'm just throwing it away and someone else in a similar situation, someone more determined, is going to take this opportunity to solve their life problems. Maybe this is the universe being kind to me. Am I making a terrible mistake by completely dismissing this?

Besides, like he said, he could have hired some hit man to do it, but he doesn't want to support criminals. He wants to help people who need it. That was why he had posted it in the caregivers section.

I step out onto the small balcony of our run-down apartment. I look down at the dead daisies I had in the pot. The neighbor below me used to complain that the flowers would fall onto her balcony. I couldn't understand that. I'd love to have flowers falling from the sky above me. She told me to get rid of the plant or she would tell the landlord. I apologized, saying I didn't mean anything by it, and I stopped watering the daisies. How did I become like this . . . so fearful . . . letting my own flowers die out of fear they might bloom and fall on the ground near my neighbor?

Part of me knows why. I gave myself away, to David, his control. I thought that was love. To let him do what he liked. To be nice to him, not challenge his fragile ego. But I was misguided. He took more than he should. And then he left. And broke me, financially.

Mary the Strong no more. Is there still warmth in the ashes of what I was once?

Could that fire ever rage again?

Across the street from my balcony, someone is loading a truck. He has one of those thick back braces to support his back when he lifts the boxes into the truck. He seems old, too old to be doing what is a young man's job, but I get it; he needs the money. He can't retire, so he works a sixty-hour week, lifting boxes of beer for frat boys to get drunk on. *You gotta do what you gotta do.*

I decide I have to take the chatting job.

I can't let the world crash down on us.

I walk back into the kitchen, sit down in front of the old Dell, and click the confirm button on the Text Co. email.

Cyril calls. I don't answer. I could ask Cyril for the money, but . . . if I go down that road, there's only so much dignity you can give away before you completely die inside.

*If you can do sex work, you can ask your boyfriend for a small loan,* a little voice inside whispers to me.

I find a vein of resilience to fight back against the voice: *It's not sex work, and he's not my boyfriend.*

I get an email back from Text Co. Someone will contact me in the next forty-eight hours to begin training. I don't like to lie to Em, but she would be devastated if she knew what I was doing to get money. So I will fudge the truth. Telemarketing, I will tell her.

Yet even if this works out, even if I earn the $300 a week, it's not enough. I need something else. I scurry around in my brain, opening one door, closing it and opening the next.

I could sell my blood.

Get another credit card.

Apply for more jobs.

Ask Cyril.

Ask David.

Check back at the library; maybe things have changed.

Shoot Eric Smith in the head and receive $100,000.

*No.*

I think and think and think. The feeling that somehow I have the solution but I'm just not thinking it through enough exhausts me. I don't have the answer. It makes me feel inadequate, useless; how is everyone else surviving?

I'm hungry. I look in the fridge and the pantry. We have no food. I have to go shopping. I just keep delaying it. And Em doesn't say anything. She practically lives on Rice Krispies.

I get an email from David. He tells me he's taking Em to New York for the tournament. He doesn't ask, just tells me. What can I do? He says I must have her ready and packed by 4:00 p.m. on Friday, doesn't say when they'll get back. He doesn't sign off; it's like he's giving instructions to a child who needs a firm hand.

How did it come to this? I loved him once. His raised chin, his determination to dominate the world that impressed me so much. I felt safe. I was alone in the world; my mother had died from cancer long ago, and my father was already in hospice by the time David came along. David was my lifeline. *I've got this*, he would say, and I knew he did. He'd come around and pick me up from my job at the aftercare place. I sought his organization, his grip on getting things done in an efficient and effective way. Now I know that he was just impatient and controlling.

I don't blame him for who he was, who he is. I blame myself. I gave the responsibility for my life to him. He wanted to take that responsibility, and I was happy to offer it. He provided for me materially, and I didn't have to worry about making the wrong decision. In return, I cooked for him, praised him, made my body available to him when he wanted it.

And then contempt started to grow in him. I don't know what the seed was that caused it. I wasn't enough anymore; my surrender wasn't enough; my body wasn't enough. He was frustrated and angry at the world. And then Emma came. He wasn't happy. The pregnancy wasn't something we had planned. That was when things really turned. I didn't have time for him as I had had before. Em was a difficult baby. I had to do everything.

David was at work, or busy, or scowling. I tore my perineum quite badly during childbirth. It took a long time to heal, and that meant we couldn't have sex. I tried other things. It felt humiliating: being on my knees, his unzipped fly, gagging as he came in my mouth. And then he'd walk off, pulling up his pants while I was left there wondering if that was what other wives did.

But it wasn't just that. I would've tolerated much more. It was that he tolerated so little, and when it came down to it, he was prepared to ruin his daughter's life because living with me was so wretched that he felt he had to divorce me. I knew of his affairs and said nothing. He knew I knew, and maybe that was why it was so difficult for him. Seeing me meant having to face the fact that he was a cheater. He couldn't handle the truth. He preferred the sweet lie that he was a nice guy in a bad marriage.

That's what kills me, that I made such an error of judgment when I met him. How could I have misread him so badly? This was a man who, under the slightest inconvenience, would leave his daughter and break up her family. I am perplexed by his lack of kindness. But it's not him I blame; that blame I save for myself. I had a chance, the first affair: I shouldn't have let it go. Where was my self-respect? I should have fought back. But I didn't. Blame and shame. My terrible twins. I hoped they would eat each other alive. But they didn't; they multiplied and had triplets—*low self-esteem, anxiety,* and *depression*.

*But that's not really you, is it? Are you not so much more?* a voice far away, as faint as a breeze, asks.

———

After a cup of black coffee, black because there is no milk, I try to manage the vortex of things swirling in my head: pay for Em's phone data for the month, read the prep manual Text Co.

has sent me, go grocery shopping, find a new job, don't shallow breathe, make sure to drink enough water. Remember to return Cyril's texts and voice messages. Phone the credit card company. Read about empowered and kind people. Remember to have Em ready for David when he comes. Remind Em about the Soller Gambit that won her the tournament in Georgia two years ago. Try not to think about the $100,000 that the thin man with tinnitus offered me if I would shoot him in the head and put him out of his misery and ensure his ailing mother would have enough money to pay for her medication.

I sit there, coffee cup in hand, still on the outside, manic on the inside. Who could give all these thoughts the attention they deserve?

*Take the $100,000.*

No.

*Take it.*

NO!

*Ping.*

Another email from Text Co. There's a tutorial. A tutorial? Really? Maybe I read this wrong; maybe this is more legit than I thought; maybe it is just lonely people looking for a "chat buddy," as the website says. Three hundred dollars a week. It said three hundred minimum, right? Maybe I can make more? Five hundred? My brain is firing now. I open the tutorial.

> Customers visit our website for stimulating conversation. There are also some customers looking to talk about their fantasies.

Hmmm.

Would that be their sexual fantasies, by any chance? Or maybe it's just their fantasies about how they would like to do good in the world. What if all these old and gray married men would like to message me about their fantasies of opening schools and soup kitchens in Africa, about how their wives don't understand that third-world education is their real passion? Is that perhaps what they mean when they say they might want to talk about their fantasies?

I read on.

- Never finish a conversation by saying things like "Good night," "Bye-bye," or "Talk later" unless the customer has taken the initiative to end the conversation for the time being.
- When the customer is about to end the conversation, always call for continued contact.

Examples include:
✔ Promise that you will message me tomorrow when you wake up.
✔ Sleep well, I will think of you (dream of you) and I can't wait to hear from you again.
✔ Next time you message me, I'll tell you a secret.

*Dream of you?* Dream of them building a school, out there in the heat of Africa, the mosquitoes, the poor sanitation, but still making sacrifices to help others?

## Pictures

Every photo the customer sends needs to be logged in this logbook. The image itself is not saved, only the explanatory text that you will write. Open the image attached to the conversation by clicking on the icon and then briefly log what the picture represents.

Example:
- Summer house, motorcycle, selfie, penis, upper body

Sorry, did they just say *penis?* Do they mean the customer will send me a photo of their penis? In Africa, while building the new school? I hope it doesn't get sunburned out there in that harsh African sun.

Gone is any pretext that this might be just a chat with a lonely person as they point out:

> If it is a photo of his penis, don't be scared. Make sure to give a lot of compliments. Men must be and are often very proud of their penises if they send a picture of them to you. Ask him what he wants you to do with it, etc. See it as an opportunity to have a good, fun conversation around it.

The earnestness around this is near absurd. *Make sure to give a lot of compliments?* Are they preschoolers bringing home a scribble of a car? Would they like me to address it directly? *Dear Mr. Penis, you are very handsome.*

A good reply message would be something like:

"Hi, thank you for the photo! You make me so hot and horny right now. It looks delicious."

My humor dies quickly. This would all be pathetic and harmless if I hadn't experienced the rage that lurks in men when their advances, however crude and juvenile, are not met with sufficient adoration for their delicate egos. There's nothing funny about a man humiliated by reality. He lashes out, usually with his fists, and normally a woman gets hurt.

I start to feel angry. I don't like these people at Text Co. anymore. At least they could have the courage to admit who they are and what they do. They should be giving a tutorial on how to deal with the trauma of seeing fathers, husbands, captains of industry, policemen, and doctors behaving like angry, spoiled children.

### Play your role and play it well.
The chat operator's job is a combination of being a creative writer and a good actor. A good operator is able to adjust his or her way of writing and overall expression so that it matches the profile of the customer who has been assigned to you for a conversation.

It is important to be able to align your writing with that of the customers' wishes, expressed in messages. A twenty-year-old girl expresses herself differently from a fifty-year-old woman. It is important to keep this in mind when writing messages.

In other words, you must not write like a fifty-year-old woman. You must appear to be a busty twenty-year-old in awe of anything the man says and turned on to the point of near orgasm just to be chatting with him.

I speed-read through the rest of the twenty-page tutorial. I'm impressed by how hard they've tried to make this all sound legitimate. I don't care anymore. I need the money, and if this is what I have to do, I'll do it to ensure my daughter's financial survival.

I know what they want.

I look at the rates again:

1000 messages → 1000 x 10 cents = 100 USD
1500 messages → 1500 x 10 cents = 150 USD
2000 messages → 2000 x 12 cents = 240 USD

Two thousand messages. What choice do I have?
*Make this work. Deal with what's in front of you.*

My mind is asking me to do a calculation I don't want to do. A morbid fascination engages my intelligence and does the math. To make $100,000, I would have to send around eight hundred thousand messages.

The numbers float in my head for a moment.

Or I could compassionately end a man's suffering and help his sick mother.

# fifteen

I'm happy because I can see that the awkwardness Em feels about spending the weekend with her father is overshadowed by the excitement she feels about going to compete at the chess tournament. She loves to compete. The challenge arises and she steps forward, her natural response being to approach it with confidence that she will beat it. It takes a Herculean effort for me not to give her a pep talk about how to try not to be overwhelmed by the occasion; how her father's new girlfriend is just that, a girlfriend, not a replacement mother with whom she has to connect; how proud we are of her, no matter how well she does in the tournament.

But I resist it all. I just hug her and tell her that I'll miss her and that she should have a great time.

I am reminded of Hafiz.

> *What is the difference*
> *Between your experience of Existence*
> *And that of a saint?*
>
> *The saint knows*
> *That the spiritual path*
> *Is a sublime chess game with God*

*And that the Beloved
Has just made such a Fantastic Move*

*That the saint is now continually
Tripping over Joy
And bursting out in Laughter
And saying, "I Surrender!"*

*Whereas, my dear,
I am afraid you still think*

*You have a thousand serious moves.*

*Em, I have no moves to make.
You will go out into the world, and I will have no moves to make.*

I manage not to cry. David hates when I do that. I've never seen him cry. Just rage. He doesn't make eye contact with me when he comes to fetch Em. He's short and terse. I wonder why he's so angry. Does he feel that being civil to me is some kind of loss to him? That maintaining his anger is the only way to win? Why is kindness so hard?

David is getting gray, and his hair is thinning. It's not a problem. It actually suits him, but I'm sure it's a growing source of frustration for him. I try to smile and be the kindness I want to see in the world, but it seems that it just makes him more irritable. I wish I could tell him that I bear him no ill will, that I hope he has a happy life, and that both our lives would be much better if we just found forgiveness for the mistakes we were too young to have handled any differently. But I can't. I wouldn't get past a few words before he would cut me off.

I wave to Chrissy in the passenger seat. Chris? She's young, of course, and she seems sweet. I'm clearly no threat to her. I try not to think about her, what she wants out of life, what she wants out of her relationship with David.

They drive off. I stand there. I hear the backing up of a truck somewhere. The streets are dirty. I should've cleaned up, I think, and then I catch myself: *I should have cleaned up the dirty streets before my ex-husband arrived to fetch our daughter?* Ridiculous. That's how crazy my mind is. It's irrational thoughts like this that give me the conviction to ignore the mad monkey inside my head. Still, though, why *are* the streets so dirty? Do they not clean here? I walk back up the stairs. I hope Em does well. If she doesn't, I hope she's able to understand that it's not a reflection of her worth in the world.

How can I teach her that?

Back at my computer, I see there are two new messages. The first is from Text Co. giving me log-in details to start finding chat buddies and sending me a number to contact them if I need any further help or have to report anything. Report anything? But I've switched off the warning alarms. I need to do this.

The other message is from my landlord. He informs me that he's unable to afford me any more leniency on this matter, and if the rent is not paid, he will have to issue an eviction notice. His tone is curt and businesslike. That was not how it started with him. He was kind and understanding, but over the months and years, with my repeated failure to pay rent on time, I have exhausted his goodwill. But I understand. He gave me my chance.

I need $500, or we will be evicted. That's around four thousand messages, four hundred a day. I can do this. I log in. I have to set up my avatar and name. I choose the animated one, a rainbow, the most innocent one I can find. I select a username: Susan, bland and homely. I go through the contacts that have been preloaded onto my account. They're all men. I look at their chatting history with the previous operator. They make no attempt to hide their desire for sexual interaction. I brush this aside and start messaging. If I could send the same message to all of them, I would save so much time. But I can't; the company checks, or so it says.

> Hey there big boy, what you up to? I feel kind of lonely, maybe we could chat for a while.
>
> I really like your profile pics. You look great. I like it when a man looks like you do.
>
> Should we chat? I'm bored and would really like that. My name is Susan. I'd love to chat with you. I'm looking for a strong man.

A strong man? Really? But I know this is no time for nuance. I put my head down and start chatting. I manage to write thirty messages before I get a response. It's from user LM352. His profile pic is a black-and-white shot of a man looking over his muscled shoulder back at me. It's cropped above the chin so you can't see his face. If he looked like this, would he really be on here? I wonder.

> Hey Susan, my cock's hard for you.

Then *ping!* He sends a picture. I recoil at the bluntness of seeing a penis. Engorged, veiny, and frightening. This is my first message. Then my notifications start pinging, three, then five, then nine. I open them up and start to speed-read. Most of them are just equally blunt and crude versions of the first. One is in such poor English that I can barely make out what is being said. And then one just says: Hello dear Susan. It is nice to meet you. Yes I would love to chat. It's from Roger3. I am struck by the politeness. I write back immediately.

Hi Roger, where are you from? What are some of your hobbies? I like . . . My first instinct is to be honest, but I am learning, so I continue, to dance and have fun. I recall the tutorial saying that you have to reply immediately and not keep the customers waiting, or they will move on. I panic, remembering the unanswered messages. I reply to the dick pics.

> Mmmm, that's huge! Oh my God, what are you going to do with that?

Ask questions, compliment them, engage.

I keep going. Like a machine. I feel nothing. I shut down all parts of me that make me human except the part required to type replies. It feels like a violation. I push the thought aside. I write things I never thought I would say. I say things as if I am writing a recipe. I feel nothing, except when Roger3 replies. He forces me to access the parts of me I have shut off to type back to the rest of these crude men. It throws me off my rhythm, breaks my typing pace.

Roger3 is asking where I grew up, if I have family around me. He sounds like a normal person just looking for a chat. But Roger3 only makes me realize how disgusting those other men are. I start to curse him in my mind. *Get out of here, Roger3. This is no place for you. Go and walk in the park; look at the flowers. Meet some normal people.* But I have no time to waste on Roger. I'm engaged in an ongoing conversation with thirteen men, all at the same time. It's impossible, and the pics are getting more graphic, and the messages are getting more vile, and one in particular is getting more violent. I feel sick, nauseous, like I'm on a merry-go-round, spinning out of control.

I realize I haven't eaten. How long have I been doing this? Hours? I look up at my kitchen window and see a bird fly past. I realize I'm holding my breath for some reason. I get up too quickly, the world spins, and I black out.

I come to sometime later to find myself lying on the floor. My head and my hip hurt. I feel weak and disoriented from the lack of food. From a deep place inside me, I also feel shame. I want to cry. Why am I failing at life so badly? But I can't give into this. If I do, I don't think I'll ever be able to come back. I hear a noise, ask myself what it is. I get up on my elbow to listen more carefully. Then I start to register that it's *ping*ing on my computer. The messages are still coming. I'm instantly overwhelmed again, flooded.

I have to eat. I crawl on the floor over to the fridge. I open it and look at the near-empty shelves. There's some strawberry jelly on the bottom rack of the door. I fumble for the jar, try to get the lid off. I'm too weak. The lid tumbles to the floor, and I put my finger into the jar and shove the jelly in my mouth. The sugar rushes through me.

# sixteen

It is as if every element of Lili's has been specifically tailored and designed exactly to Eric's taste. The cream cloth; the dark mahogany wood; the crystal; the silver; the violin player; the water fountain; the white lilies; the waitstaff, young and flirty, just how Eric likes them; and the food, each dish an elegant masterpiece of taste and texture and class.

It's the one place where Eric feels at home. The unpleasantness of the real world, with its foul smells and ugly people, can't touch him. He likes to joke with the owners, Tyrell and Sid, that they should make the ugly people pay a cover charge.

Mark has brought them here for Eric's forty-eighth birthday. They're on their second bottle of Chateau Montelena, and for a moment, Eric wonders if he should really go through with his drastic plan. Mark, of course, knows nothing about it, and seeing him here, being together, happy, surrounded by the opulence and easy laughter of the wealthy, Eric has to consider if a bullet to the head is really the answer to his problem.

But he knows that this is the chardonnay talking. He's been through this before. This is not a new idea or a new plan. How long has he been suffering? What happens when lunch at Lili's is over and they have to go home again? Is Mark really capable of making Eric forget his daily pain? No, of course he isn't, and a lunch at Lili's is an anomaly. This is not how his life really is: flitting from a late lunch, shopping at JJ Malibu, and then attending a party at the house of Fiona, Mark's famous actress friend. In fact, this day is the very reason why Eric has decided to do what he must. These days are not his life. These days are only a cruel reminder of the life he doesn't have, the life he deserved but has not been given.

Now Mark is flirting with the young waiter, Steve. Steve with his tight shirt and his deep tan. He's got his hand on Mark's shoulder as he cackles like a housewife at Mark's weak joke about "hot buns." Yet instead of jealousy, Eric just feels depressed. A wasted life. He has tried so long, worked so hard, made the effort, put in the hours, been kind and present; he's shown up, blown $1,200 on some positive-thinking seminar. He has done it all, but still, nothing worked out.

But soon, soon this will be over . . . Soon his suffering will be over.

Eric fakes a smile, makes a comment to Steve about his white teeth, and now all three of them are laughing and flirting with each other. By the time the Tahitian vanilla cake arrives, Eric feels a headache coming on and doesn't want to go shopping at JJ Malibu anymore, nor does he want to go to Fiona's party with all her fabulously famous friends. They drive home in silence.

Mark is being a good sport about it, but Eric knows he's been looking forward to going out. It has been so long since they did anything, and now, jacked up on expensive wine and titillated hormones, he's trying not to be resentful. Eric sees this, but he couldn't care less. His mood has soured. He's tempted to start a fight. *Do you even care about me?* But he resists. This will soon be over if that sad woman would just call already. Eric resolves that if he hasn't heard from her by tomorrow, he'll make contact again.

And then he needs to get the gun.

# seventeen

I wanted to be a writer when I was growing up. I loved reading and getting lost in the words the authors had put together. The world created by almost any book was always better than the one I was living in. It was not that my life was so terrible. It was just that the books didn't have the harsh edge of real life. Books had happy endings. The girl got the guy, the monster was defeated, and the dog made it back home.

I took some solace from that.

Then I started writing. I started creating a world that I could live in; a world where I could escape from having to see the worry in my mother's eyes when my father didn't come home, escape from the hockey coach who used to rub my back when he talked to me. I used the words like little bricks, to build myself a fort wherein I could hide from the war outside.

I wrote a story about a little girl who saved a cat in a tree. The cat revealed that she could talk to the little girl, and they became friends, and the cat would tell the girl about what was happening in the rest of the neighborhood. It won a prize, the Skippingstone Youth Award for the best fiction story for ages ten to thirteen. I got into poems too, but they weren't very good.

I started a novel in my twenties about a woman who went to Africa to care for orphans. She rescued a young girl from prostitution and fell in love with an African man, but they had to elope because the boy's traditional parents disowned him because he wanted to marry a foreigner. They escaped to Thailand with the young girl and . . . Well, I still haven't finished it yet.

And then I read the great poet Hafiz:

> *Even*
> *After*
> *All this time*
> *The sun never says to the earth,*
> *"You owe Me."*

And the mystic writings of the Vedas:

*And then He walked on the land and underfoot the stones melted in love at his touch and then He smiled and all the flowers bloomed.*

That young girl, the last remnants of hope still trying to take root in her heart, what would she think if she saw me now, many years later, sitting at the wobbly kitchen table, her fingers cramping as she punches out: Yes, you can take me hard from behind big daddy and That's the biggest one I've ever seen and What do you plan to do with me now? I log out for the night. I see I've sent 286 messages. That's about thirty dollars.

I'll never be able to keep up this pace.

———

I wake up the next day and call Em. She won her pool games. She's playing the quarterfinal at 10:00 a.m. and then, if she wins, the semifinal at 1:00 p.m. I can watch online, she tells me. I ask her how things are with David. She pauses. I know that pause.

*Okay, I guess,* she says.

Would David ever transfer his anger to her? Would his contempt for me mutate into a contempt for her? I shudder. I feel a dormant rage, simmering in a place long forgotten. If he ever . . . I don't finish the thought. I feel something stir deep inside. Mary the Strong blinks her long-closed eyes.

I wish her well and tell her I'll watch online.

*Good luck, sweetie. Win or lose, I love you.*

I get back to my chat buddies. I feel dirty straightaway, the hard edge of reality sticking in my side as I type away to the sad men, so aggressive and so vile. Eventually I manage to shut down the part affected by what I'm writing and reading, and I get back into my automatic state. But in the recesses of my mind, I know I can't go on. I know I cannot spend my hours and days like this, with these people who are so desperate to exploit me.

---

Cyril calls. I don't answer. He leaves a message. He wants to take me out to eat tonight. His message is sweet and friendly. I'm struck by what normal men sound like. I don't want to go. I know he will want something more. Men and sex, was this once a beautiful thing? The images and words of Text Co. blink through my mind.

I ignore his message. I log in to the link to watch Emma's game. My Wi-Fi connection is weak, and the stream is glitched and freezes regularly, but I can still follow the game.

Em starts poorly. Her opponent is a teenager named Francesca Simon from Seattle. She's a very aggressive player and captures Em's king pawn before they are even out of the blocks. But Em is thoughtful and patient. She consolidates, castles, barricades up her king, and locks down a defensive position.

Francesca gets impatient because of the lack of options for attack. Em sets her up by offering an easy pawn. Francesca can't resist and takes the pawn, but Em swoops in and takes her bishop. Francesca rushed in and got caught.

Em makes a carefully considered play on the right flank. Francesca is rattled by Em's slow and deliberate style and starts playing recklessly. Em traps Francesca's queen. It's a critical move. Francesca is left scrambling. But then I see Em looking at Francesca.

*No!* I say to the empty kitchen.

Francesca looks sad, and Em sees it.

*Take her down!* I shout at the screen. But I know what is going on. I've seen this too often. Em feels bad for Francesca. Empathy slowly and gently leads the Killer out of the room and sits down in its place next to Emma. It's Emma the Empathic now, not Emma the Killer, facing off against Francesca Simon.

Em takes her foot off Francesca's neck, plays a few innocuous moves. Francesca sees the gap and goes in hard to recover her position. By the time Em has realized that Francesca's coming for her, it's almost too late. I watch her wake up, knock Empathy out of the way, and scurry to regain her dominance. The endgame is a frantic mess. Two young, inexperienced girls who have lost their heads, both slugging away wildly and desperately for a knockout blow.

They stalemate, and it's a tie. They have to flip a coin. Em calls heads. It's tails. Francesca goes through. I can see Em's face, furrowed brow, confused at how she lost, confused at the misstep her kindness took her to; but worst of all is seeing that there's a part of her moving toward acceptance, like loss might just be her lot, as if that is perhaps what she should come to expect from her life. My stomach knots. I can barely tolerate that I have done that to myself, but to see my twelve-year-old daughter, so young, starting to accept such a life . . . And then I'm going to hold you down and drill you like the bitch you are, says the message fading on the top right of my screen.

Fuck you, I write back in rage.

What did you say?

I realize I'm going to lose my job.

More parts of me die as I write back: Sorry, that should have read, fuck me.

He buys it. Damn right I'm going to fuck you, bitch.

I can't do this. This is not a life.

# eighteen

> I'm dropping her off at 10. She lost.

It's a text from David. She didn't lose; it was a stalemate. Is he upset with her? Does he feel Emma has in her what he so despises about me? Does he feel the need to berate it out of her? Can he even articulate his constant anger?

I realize that I have no dinner for her. Just then, Cyril texts:

> Checking in . . . you up for a bite to eat?

Cyril. I like Cyril. He would come and deliver the new books at the library. I noticed how kindly and gently he dealt with the old man who helped him take stock. I liked the way he shyly complimented my dress. I like Cyril, even though it's not the way he would hope.

I'll go. I'll nibble at my food and bring the rest home for Em.

> That sounds nice, thank you, I text back. He responds immediately with two red heart emojis.

I bathe. The steam fogs up the small room. I realize how

tired I am, how much the Text Co. job is taking out of me, how much my anxiety is draining me. At the same time, something keeps gnawing at my mind that I have forgotten . . . I rack my brain. What is it? It feels important, something I shouldn't forget, but I can't remember.

I fall asleep in the bath and dream I'm lying in the middle of the street at night and it's pouring rain. I'm lying on my stomach, my cheek on the cold, wet asphalt as thick raindrops explode around me. The reflections of streetlights in the puddles shatter with each raindrop. Tears are running from my eyes, but I'm not crying. I stare across the road at the warm lights of a restaurant. Through the fogged-up windows, I see a strip club of some sort. I see the men's faces leer with lust at a girl standing on a stage. She's young, too young to be doing this. I feel horror. The young girl is Em.

I wake with a splash, my heart beating wildly. It's a horrible, horrible dream. I want to cancel dinner. I can't go out. I don't have it in me to get changed and make small talk and be anxious the whole time, knowing that Cyril will want to kiss me. And then I remember the food. I've barely eaten, and Em's going to be back soon. I text Cyril and ask him to let me know when he arrives, and I will come downstairs. I can't face him seeing my apartment.

When he texts, I go downstairs and am surprised to see he's not alone. He's with Jaya, Cyril's older brother. I've met him before at one of Cyril's plays. Jaya is in his late fifties. He was a Hare Krishna monk for thirty years, Cyril told me. He was a spiritual teacher and used to lecture around the world and take on students, and then something happened. I'm not sure of the details. He's staying in Cyril's spare room at the moment and grows vegetables at a local co-op.

He's very big, and sitting in the back seat of the car, he seems even bigger with his broad shoulders hunched over. He has gray hair but a sweet smile like a young boy. I don't know why, but I like him. Cyril is dropping him off at an NA meeting. He's a counselor there a few nights a week.

Jaya greets me by name and asks me how everything is in my life. I struggle not to break down right there in the car. It must be his ex-monk vibe that makes me want to confess. Instead, I just reply, *Fine, thanks, and you?*

He smiles and says, *You know, fighting the good fight.*

What fight? I want to ask him immediately. Suddenly, it seems urgent that I know what he's talking about. It seems crucial. What fight? Is there a good fight? But I don't say anything, and now Cyril is pulling over and we're dropping Jaya off.

There is a strength in not fighting. It's a paradox, but it has always been clear to me that most fighting is just a fragile ego so afraid that they could possibly be wrong that they'll fight to the death rather than admit someone else might be right. So to not fight, to try to see where one could be at fault and as such adjust and grow from that, has always seemed to me like an act of bravery.

But sometimes one *must* fight. Sometimes people will take advantage of you if you don't. That's how Mary the Strong became Mary the Weak.

Is that "fighting the good fight"?

Em is vegetarian, so I have to order something that she will eat, or this whole venture will have been a waste of time. And I have to make sure the portion is big enough that I can eat something so as not to upset Cyril but still leave enough for Em. I settle on an Indian curry with naan bread and spring rolls. Cyril smiles as I reel off my hearty order to the indifferent waitress.

Cyril seems surprised that I have agreed to join him tonight. I try to be friendly and interested in his life. He talks about the new *Fast & Furious* movie coming out. He says his friend at the improv club has a brother who's an extra in the movie. He's so excited about it. He thinks that Dwayne "the Rock" Johnson is underrated.

*Did you see him in Rampage?*

*Um, no, I don't think so.*

*So, so good. He's got range. People just see his muscles. If you watch his eyes, he's pretty good, same as Stallone. People just think he's a jock, but did you know he wrote Rocky, and it was nominated for an Oscar for Best Screenplay?*

*Really?*

*Yeah, people underestimate him.*

I look at Cyril. The part of me that can engage in this type of small talk is empty. I don't think I have a single word left. Silence sits over us. I don't mind it. Yes, it's uncomfortable, but that's just life, most of the time: uncomfortable. And uncomfortable is better than agonizing.

*You're not hungry?*

*I was, but my stomach feels a little off. I'll eat the rest later. It was delicious, though.*

I tell him that Em is getting back from New York, and I've got to get home. I hope he doesn't mind. He remarks: *She seems brainy, like a scientist or something.*

My heart swells. I unexpectedly find a smile. Cyril smiles back. Cyril is kind.

We drive back in silence, but it's not that uncomfortable anymore. I realize that Cyril's hesitancy with me is his sensitivity. After dealing with such crass men all day long at Text Co., I notice and value his gentleness. I kiss him when he drops me off. It's a light kiss on the cheek, almost out of gratitude for his kind words about Emma, but also because he's not vile.

*Dear men of the world. That's how you get a woman. Kindness. Not dick pics.*

---

Emma is tired and crabby when she gets back. I don't pry. I don't mention the stalemate. I don't ask about David or Chris, Chrissy? She's not hungry, so I eat the leftover curry myself. While she showers, I open the Dell. There is a message from the Text Co. admin. Whatever algorithm they are using is telling them my relationships and clients are moving on to new chat buddies too quickly. Chat buddies—that's what they call us. *Sex workers* is too on the nose, I guess. Matt5, the admin, suggests I try to better match their style of language.

I'm not slutty enough, is what they're saying. They also encourage me to up my output and remind me of the next bonus level if I do so. I don't want to increase my output. I don't want to maintain my output. I never want to open the site again, but I need the money. I'll push on until I can't take it anymore, and then . . . I don't know. I don't even want to think about that.

Em goes to bed early. The tournaments take it out of her, I know. It's not just the prolonged focus; it's the competing too. She has to fight against her conciliatory nature. That's tiring.

I stare at the old Dell screen and try to find the switch that turns me into a machine without feelings or dignity. I start chatting, managing to exert the least amount of mental attention on what I'm writing. My mind drifts. There is still that annoying feeling that I have forgotten something important rubbing up against me. What is it? I strain to remember.

I'm tired and bored at the same time. I picture myself floating out of my body, looking down at this woman, writing these things to keep food on the table.

Are these the stories I thought I would end up telling with my life?

> My panties are wet.

> Yeah, how wet?

> So wet I am sliding off my chair.

There's a pause before he replies. I can tell he's not sure what to say. I laugh at the thought of his small brain trying to figure out whether I'm making fun of him.

> I think I fractured my coccyx from the fall.

> What?

Are you hard? I write back quickly before he can register my contempt for all this.

> Like a rock!

Not too smart, this one.

# nineteen

*Mom, Mom, wake up.*

I have fallen asleep at the kitchen table. Em is there, ready for school. She has a confused look on her face.

*What are you doing?*

I take a moment to come to my senses. I wipe the drool from my cheek.

*What is this?*

I see her face. It's not confusion; it's shame. She's pointing at the browser and all the messages. I realize what she's seeing, what she's reading! Panic surges like an electric current through me. I'm immediately very awake.

*It's not what you think.*

But she's crying now. Confused, angry tears. She's storming out the house, and I am running after her.

*Em, wait, please let me explain.*

*Leave me alone!*

She's shouting. The neighbor on the first floor is watching. I'm in my sweats with a thin shirt and no bra, barefoot. I cover up with my arms.

*Em, please!*

But I know she won't stop. I watch her go. I'm shaking from the adrenaline of panic. Seconds ago I was in a deep sleep, and now I'm standing in the middle of the sidewalk, trying to shout after my daughter, who has seen her mother engaging in pornographic chats with strangers.

Two joggers run past. I smile weakly as they nod, and then a car pulls up and a woman gets out. She has a stone face and thick legs and is dressed in a black skirt and a white blouse. She carries a clipboard. When she walks into the apartment complex, I see the logo on her briefcase. DCF.

DCF? Why do I know that logo? A memory bubbles up of an email I received some time ago.

And then I remember the thing I've been trying to recall: The Department of Children and Families is coming to inspect our living conditions. On the thirtieth. My brain realizes that's today.

She's here. Now.

I run after her.

*Hello, sorry, miss.*

She stops and turns. She looks at me and I wither.

*Yes?*

I contemplate lying to her, telling her I'm Mary's sister and Mary said she was sorry but she had to run out, so could they reschedule for tomorrow?

*I am, um . . . I think you're here to see me.*

*Are you Mary Williams?*

I wish I had lied.

*Yes.*

She nods.

*My name is Serena James. From Child and Family Services. Please, can you show me your apartment?*

*Okay.*

She's looking at my clothes, my bare feet. She follows me as we walk up the stairs to my apartment. The door is still open from when I ran after Em. We walk inside to the kitchen. I'm making excuses for the state of the place, telling her it's not normally like this, apologizing for not being better prepared, trying to explain how I forgot about the appointment. I'm rambling, flustered, and then I notice that she's not looking at me. She's looking at the screen of the old Dell, open on the kitchen table.

By the time I register what is happening, it's too late. *Plunger69* has sent me a clip of someone masturbating, complete with exaggerated animal grunts. The clip is playing on a loop on my computer's open Text Co. page. For a moment, the representative of Child and Family Services just looks at me, like she's confused as to how I've been allowed to keep my child for as long as I have. I stare back at her with no words, unable to even begin to explain anything.

My chest is tightening. The shame is squeezing at me with such force that I'm worried that I'm going to have a heart attack. My worst fears are manifesting before my eyes.

I'm free-falling, tumbling head over heels. It's as if I've been climbing up a mountain my whole life with tiny incremental progress, occasionally stopping for many weeks to rest, before climbing another inch upward, all the while watching others barge past me, making huge strides toward the top of their lives. The climbing is an exertion that is taking everything I have. I am cut and bruised and beaten by every inch of the ascent, and then out of nowhere a single violent gust of wind comes, and I'm falling, down and down, hurtling toward the ground below. Just how far will I drop? Just how far reaching will the consequences of this act of cruel providence be? Will David ever let me see Em again? Will this be made public? Will this shame finally make me lose my mind?

Serena James has seen more than she needs to. I have no way of explaining that this is what I have to do to stop us from falling into homelessness. She sees a soiled take-out box on the kitchen table. The turmeric-and-cream sauce has congealed into a dirty brown smudge over the white containers. She looks in the fridge and sees it's almost empty: a half gallon of milk, some mustard, and the open strawberry-jelly jar with a spoon that I never packed away. She sees the Rice Krispies in the pantry and a tin of tomatoes.

Ms. James has a concerned look on her face. Her expression says that maybe I'm a dangerous person. She visibly tenses as she continues her inspection. I want to plead with her; to try to explain how much I love Em. I want to apologize. I know it shouldn't be like this. But I am mortified. I'm free-falling. I am stunned by the sudden drop of altitude. She asks what work I do. I look at her for far too long before answering in a small broken voice.

*I don't have a job anymore.*

She writes something on her clipboard.

*Ms. James, please. Can I explain?*

But she won't have any of this. She's seen people like me before.

*The office will make contact with you once the report has been filed. Thank you for your time this morning, Ms. Williams.*

It's not what you think! Please, can you just give me a chance to explain.

But she's already leaving. I want to run after her, shake her, get in her face. *This is not right. This is not my fault!* But I don't. I stand there. I can't go out like this again, no shoes, no bra, wild hair, chasing after the family-services woman. I stand there, alone in the kitchen. But I'm not standing. I'm still falling. I know there is some way to go before I hit the bottom.

# twenty

Hope is the last thing to die. This comes from the title of an Auschwitz survivor's memoir. It's a horrific story of the unbearable suffering she underwent in the concentration camps. Despite the rapes, the torture, and the loss of humanity, she described how ultimately, she had hope, and that hope was what kept her alive in spite of everyone dying around her.

I'm lying on the kitchen floor, crying. I'm crying because part of me feels my hope is dead. And I know that if my hope dies, I truly will have nothing. I have to get up. I have to find a way to breathe the next breath, take the next step, speak the next word. But I can't. I'm paralyzed by the shame and fear and disappointment at myself. How could I not be?

The morning passes as I lie still on the kitchen floor. I feel the life I once had slowly receding away, becoming a vague, distant memory on a foggy day. I don't have the energy to hold on to it; I have no will to do so.

I just want to let it go.

I'm giving up this exhausting business of trying to stay afloat, and instead, I let the ocean of failure take me down,

down,
>    down,
>        down,
>            into
>                oblivion.

And then I think of Em.

It's like an electric shock of clarity. She will be home soon. It jolts me out of my funk. I'm on my feet. What am I going to tell her about what she saw? What am I going to tell her about Ms. James? I stand, somehow finding the will to take the next step, to do something, anything.

Dear Em,

    I am sorry for what you saw. I always felt that my job has been to try and protect you from the suffering of the world, but I realize I can't do that. I don't have that capacity. I realize nobody can do that. In trying to keep you from the suffering of the world, I've had to lie to you about things. I can't keep lying. Perhaps trying to help you deal with suffering will be a better strategy than my unsuccessful attempt to protect you from it.

    The truth is even before I was let go from the library, I've been drowning in debt that I don't know if I'll ever be able to get out of. I have no money. Out of desperation, I took a job messaging crude men what they wanted to hear. It made me feel sick, but at this stage I've been unable to find any other work.

    Unfortunately, this is not the worst part of it. The Department of Children and Families has become aware of the work I'm doing and my inability to provide a proper home for you financially. It looks like you may have to live with David until I'm able to sort this out. I know this is difficult to hear, but you will survive these things and you will become resilient and capable of handling the world.

I'm sorry for my role in all of this. I love you more than anything in this world, and I'm prepared to do whatever I can to be there for you. We have already been through so much together, and you're not only my beautiful daughter but also my precious friend. I hope this is understandable. I hope one day to be the mother you deserve.

Love,<br>Mom

The letter is written with detachment and clarity. I have no idea where it comes from. Is this my hysterical strength?

As I finish the letter, I receive an incoming text that pings on my phone:

> Dearest Mary, someone has agreed to help me with my problem, although I don't feel very comfortable with him. If, however, he's the only person who will assist me, I'll go ahead, as I know I cannot continue much longer in this state of pain. By any chance would you reconsider helping me? I would greatly appreciate it if we could perhaps meet at least one more time, and I could explain what it would entail and see if I could make you more comfortable about helping not only me but my mother too. Kindly, Eric Smith.

The value of the money he is offering has increased tenfold in the last twenty-four hours.

One hundred thousand dollars.

Is this the solution? Is this the answer to my prayers? That money would solve everything.

I see a light at the end of the tunnel.

And then I remember what he's asking me to do.

He wants me to shoot him in the head. I cannot do that, I know that. Only a psychopath could do that. I deflate again. Like a sad balloon. I stare at his text message.

Kindly, Eric Smith.

Is he kind? Would this be kindness? To shoot a man in the head?

*One hundred thousand dollars . . .* whispers a voice from somewhere.

# twenty-one

Eric sees her walking through the Waffle House parking lot. She looks worse than when they first met. This is good, he thinks. He knows that what he's asking someone to do is an extreme thing and that it's going to take someone at a desperate point in their life for them to actually consider doing this. He knows that he can't trust a criminal to do it. He needs someone who will follow his instructions; that's crucial. He can't have a reckless person. Things can't go wrong. A nonfatal wound? Eric shudders at the thought.

She enters through the front door. He stands gingerly and offers a polite smile. They sit at the same booth as before. Eric has calculated this; it creates familiarity. That makes her feel at ease. Close up she looks worse than he thought. He speaks slowly and softly:

*I just want to say thank you so much for coming. It's been . . .* Eric swallows. *It's been hard.*

He orders some coffee. When she agrees to a cup, Eric knows she's coming around. She wouldn't be sitting here and having a cup of coffee in a second meeting if this were not something she was seriously contemplating. He takes his time, being very gentle, careful not to push too hard or too fast. He talks thoughtfully, like he's dealing with a wounded animal. She's fragile, and he knows a single wrong word could make her bolt. What happened to her? He wonders. She was probably a mildly attractive and happy person at some stage in her life. He shows her a picture of his mother.

*She's seventy-eight. She raised me and my four sisters by herself.*

Mary looks at the photograph—the thick-set, competent woman smiling back at her, crocheting a scarf. It's an old photograph, from the days before digital. Some of the colors bleed over the corner at the bottom of the photograph.

*When I tried to do it myself last time . . .*

She frowns. Eric realizes she doesn't follow—that he's being too cryptic.

*When I tried to kill myself with pills before . . .*

Mary's eyes widen.

*. . . my mother came to see me at the hospital and told me she understood. She knows . . . the pain of it all.*

He takes a sip of his lukewarm coffee. He needs to do this, needs to give her time to digest the implications of this act. That his mother would understand what he wants Mary to do.

*She looks like a kind person.*

*She is.*

And then Mary Williams steps over a threshold that Eric has been patiently waiting for her to cross for the last few days.

*I just don't know how I could do this. I mean, how would it happen?*

He wants to pump his fist. Yes, she's in! There is still some surface hesitancy, but he knows, somehow, somewhere, something has shifted in her head, and now the reality of the money will be too strong for her to resist.

*I have it all worked out, Mary. This isn't something I've taken lightly at all,* he explains in a slow and thoughtful voice. *I have applied hours and hours of thought and consideration to how this could be done in the easiest and simplest way, for someone like you to help me.*

He goes in for the kill.

*The moment I saw you, I could tell you were a compassionate person. If I was ever going to get help with this, it would be from a person like you.*

Mary looks at him for a long moment. And then she looks down, seemingly resigned to what he senses is her only option for survival.

*Okay, can you explain to me how it would be done?*

# twenty-two

The bus jostles my shoulders as it drives over a bump in the road. I stare through the window as downtown streaks by like a smudge on the dirty glass. I see a young mother with her baby in a stroller. She's sitting on a bench and gazing lovingly at the sleeping child. The bus comes to a stop at a light. I look down at a man and his car. He's got an open gym bag on the back seat. I look at the deodorant can and some crumpled shorts inside. I know what I'm doing. I'm trying not to think about what Eric said at the Waffle House, the details of it, the ease of it, how well thought out it was. He had planned everything. I'm trying not to think about the $200,000. Yes, he doubled it; he said he understood how it might be harder for me than it seemed to him.

Two hundred thousand dollars.

He has it all worked out. I didn't want to hear the plan. It made it sound too real and too easy. But I heard it, a simple plan for me to get $200,000. It goes like this: I take an Uber to a nearby coffee shop that is open late at night. Instead of going into the coffee shop, I walk one block to his house. I walk around to the unlocked back door. I take the gun with a silencer from the inside drawer of the kitchen counter, I walk into the bedroom next to the living room, and I shoot him three times. I walk out the house, taking a bag of $200,000 sitting at the doorway, and go home and create the life that Emma and I fully deserve.

I try not to think about this. I try to think about the couple riding on the electric scooter in the bike lane next to the bus. I try to think about their happy life. I try to think about the old man in the front of the bus, doing a crossword puzzle on a folded newspaper. I try to think about the pigeon with one foot hopping on the sidewalk.

But I can't.

All I can think about is the bag with the $200,000.

The bus comes to my stop, and I get out. I've left the letter for Em on the kitchen table. She should be home from school by now. She should have read it. I tense, my cortisol-flooded body flushed with another dose. I walk up the stairs to my apartment. There's a puddle of brown water in the hallway. What is that? Was that there when Ms. James came? Another shard of shame digs into my back. The paint is peeling on the ceiling above the apartment door. Was that there too?

Em is in the bedroom. I can see she's read the letter by its new position on the kitchen table. I walk into her room.

She's lying on the bed, on her side, with her back to me. I walk over to her, sit on the edge of the bed, and put my hand on her shoulder. We sit like that for a bit, and then she turns over and looks at me. She's been crying. My heart breaks, but I try not to show it.

*I don't want to live with Dad.*

*I know*, I think. *I know better than anybody else alive, dear Em, what kind of man he is. I know his rages, his frustrations, his blame, the dissatisfaction, his control, his manipulations. I know he feels guilty for breaking up the family; I know how this all comes out in his unhealthy attempts to indulge you. I know how uncomfortable you feel when he does that, the inherent father-daughter bond contaminated by his guilt. I know, Em, I know, I know, my sweet child.*

I think all these things but say nothing. I just look at the sweet, innocent young girl, forced to face adult pain at such a tender age.

I can feel the anxiety building, growing inside me, seeping into every one of my cells and threatening to saturate me. I want to scream and rage . . . but I manage a reasonable tone.

*I don't know what will happen.*

This is the burden of love. Em does this to me. My ability to cope with the world and function in a rational and positive way, to find solutions, to remain hopeful, is all heightened around her. So, in spite of the mania starting to gear up and the lightness in my stomach starting to churn, I somehow manage to keep it together.

*The person who came from the state . . . There was no food in the house. I forgot to go shopping, and—*

*We have food to eat.* She's protesting, close to tears.

*It's not just the food. The chatting job, it was a mistake. I don't have another job yet.*

*It's not fair,* she says, her face crumpling up, hot with pain and anger.

*It isn't, but even if you have to go, it won't be permanent.*

*How do you know? How do you know I won't have to live there forever?*

I don't know.

---

The next morning I wake up and see Emma still in bed. She does not want to go to school. She says she doesn't feel great.

She's not sick; she's sad. I don't question it and let her stay home. I get a message from Text Co. telling me that unless I increase my output, I am going to lose my customers and be relegated to a lower tier.

There's also an email from the Department of Children and Families. I have to go to a court hearing with the judge on Friday.

He's going to get her. I don't know how I know this, but I do. This isn't an opinion. This is a fact. I can't fight him. I don't have that in me.

I notice the Bhagavad Gita on the table. The warrior Arjuna on the cover didn't want to fight either. Do I have to fight David? Is that my only recourse? I wonder if there's some part of me that could actually pull the trigger of the gun that Eric Smith will place in his kitchen drawer. In how many novels have I read this? The character raises the gun, points it at the target, and pulls the trigger. Sometimes the book describes the look of horror on the other character's face as they've been shot and then the slow look down at the gut and the dramatic pause before the shirt blooms in the red flower of blood.

And then I take the bag full of money next to the front door and leave.

The bag full of money.

Bam, bam.

Take the bag.

Gone girl gone.

I scratch around in the room of my mind for a solution other than this. It's like looking for a large gray mammal inside a room with an elephant in it. I look in the drawers, under the rug, behind the curtains; I look everywhere but at the large gray elephant standing in the middle of the room. I know it's there. I'm looking in the hope that I can find another large gray solution to my impending homelessness that does not involve shooting a man. But the more I look, the more I realize there is no other solution.

Bam! Bam!

Take the bag full of money.

Problem solved.

# twenty-three

Mark is washing the dishes. He cooked dinner at his house. He made puff pastries with spinach and feta and sun-dried tomatoes. But he didn't use enough butter in the pastries, so they were dry and bland. He's apologizing. Eric feels guilt circle him like a beaten dog, looking for a way in. He wonders if there is some other solution than what he's planned. But he's run through the scenarios so many times in his head. Mark has tried so hard. He's always known Eric's pain. He always tried to make everything better. *I'm sorry, Mark; if only there were some other way, but I don't know it.*

Eric watches Mark, with his *Can Be Bribed with Wine* apron. He looks like a young boy from behind. Eric thinks he's drinking too much these days. It's his own pain.

*Something's going on, isn't it?* Mark asks him.

*Nothing.* But Eric knows he needs something more here.

*It's just . . .* He pauses, like he's trying to find the right way to express these things he's feeling inside.

*It's just . . . I realized you love me, and that makes me very happy.*

Mark's eyes widen; his brow crinkles, and then he blinks back a tear as he looks at Eric.

*Oh, honey... that's so sweet.*

Watching Mark, Eric can't help but feel that he will be glad when this is over. Breaking up with Mark would have been messy, and it would have been exhausting to have to deal with the breakdown that surely would follow. Mark is too emotional, too sentimental; he would never understand. He has come over to Eric's side of the table now. He has Eric's face in his hands as he stares earnestly into his eyes.

*I do love you. I love you more than anything in the world.* Then he says with a spring in his voice, *Let me get some more wine.*

Eric stares at the crinkly pastry on his plate. He sticks a finger into the corner of the pastry. It crumbles into dry shards on the white plate. Like a shattered dream, the dream of what he thought they would become. It will soon be over. Eric has resigned himself to this. He's resigned to the drastic steps that he has to take. He knows that he cannot go on like this anymore. He feels sadness but also something else: exhilaration...

His meeting with Mary could not have gone better. He took a risk, but it was calculated. He remembers last year when he found Louise. She was clearly the right kind of person to do this, but he can now see where he made his mistake. Yes, she was desperate for the money, but his error was that he gave her too much time between her initial agreement to his request and the actual day she had to do it. Louise started to think too much, started to ask too many questions, and eventually she told her oldest son about it and asked him to help her, and that was when Eric knew it was over. He cut her off like an infected limb. He learned from that. He knew that he couldn't make the same mistake with Mary. He told her she had to tell him by Friday—two days from now—and then, if she was committed, she must do it on that Sunday. It was now or never.

And she didn't panic. He led her deeper and deeper into the

cave, her eyes adjusting to the darkness of what he was asking her to do. This absurd thing he was asking was starting to sound reasonable. She's going to do it, he's sure.

Mark wants Eric to stay the night. He's drunk and emotional. Eric thinks, why not, a last hurrah. They might as well squeeze whatever last pleasures they can out of this doomed relationship.

# twenty-four

I sit in the judge's chambers with David and his lawyer and my state-appointed counsel. Her office is stuffy and cramped. Papers are overflowing on the judge's small desk; boxes and files are on the floor. And she looks mean, not the kind, wise matriarch dispensing wisdom and guidance that you see in the movies.

My body is vibrating with fear and shame and anticipation as the judge, glasses on her nose, reads some papers. Is this a list of all my faults, the faults David has told her I have, the faults Ms. James, the Children and Families officer, has noted down? I tried to speak to my state-sponsored attorney earlier, but he was distracted, as if he were desperately trying to prepare for a case that he had only just been informed of, only to then have me asking him about my case, which he was equally bewildered about. But then his phone rang and suddenly he was laughing, telling the person on the other end of the line that he was *dropping G's, bro, dropping G's, that's how we roll here.*

The dream is getting confusing again. Who is this person? *Gotta bounce, bro.*

The judge looks up from her papers. She stares at me. I wonder if David knows what Ms. James saw, heard. Is it written in those papers, what his ex-wife is doing in his child's home? I wonder how this dream will end. Maybe it's a drowning dream. That's how it feels, like I'm drowning, not in water but in a thick, heavy, wet blanket of shame.

The judge looks down at the papers again, like she's trying to reconcile what she is reading with the person sitting in front of her.

My state-appointed attorney is texting furiously on his phone. He's intense. I feel all his pent-up energy pulsating within him. He's young, too young; his body needs to be active. I wonder how long he'll be able to stay sitting in the chair before he has to move.

David has his jaw set. His lawyer smiles at me. Nothing makes any sense.

And now the judge is addressing me. There's a sternness in her voice, and what she's saying is damning. With every sentence, she places a thick, heavy blanket of shame on my shoulders. She moves quietly and meditatively. This is my punishment, to bear the weight of this. And the blankets keep coming, even though my frail shoulders can barely take the weight and my thin legs threaten to buckle.

*If, over time, Ms. Williams, you are able to create a safe and caring environment for your child to live with you, the court would be willing to reconsider this judgment, but as of today Emma will be in the custody of her father.*

The lawyers rise, and I take a moment to realize I should stand as well, and then the judge leaves. Before I can say anything, my attorney has left too. David tells me he will fetch Em from school and that I should pack her belongings. He'll send someone to fetch them later. And then they leave, and I am left alone in the chambers. I sit back down.

I stare into the middle distance, and after a period of time I am unaware of, I make the decision that I will shoot Eric Smith like he asked me to, and I will use that money to create a safe and caring environment for my daughter, just as the judge has instructed.

My head swims. I feel like I'm stoned. I drift out of the judge's chamber and walk down the corridor. I don't know where I'm going.

*Hey, bitch!*

Someone is shouting at me. He's a tall, scruffy man with a baseball cap on backward and grease on his jeans. He's running toward me now, yelling, *You're a whore, a fucking whore!*

He's crashing into me. I'm knocked against the bench on the side of the corridor. I fall back in slow motion, bewildered by this as I am bewildered by everything. But the angry man is not coming for me; he's trying to grab the woman next to me. There are security guards grabbing at the angry man now. They're trying to separate him from the woman. People nearby are screaming.

I'm on the floor, and there's chaos around me. Fists fly; people shout; a potted plant has been knocked over and broken, its dark soil spilling over the cream tiled floor like a stain on humanity's civility. The angry man is being tased. I see a blue vein throb on his forehead as his body shakes and shudders as if possessed by a demon. The police and security guards take control. The woman he was going after is standing over him now, shouting, *Y'all just a dumb crackhead. Look at you now! You come for me, you get hell. Y'all a dumb junkie. Look at you now. Ha ha ha.*

I lie there. I stare. Everything is moving too fast for me. I decide it's better to just lie here for a moment. I can't undo what has happened, but if I can at least stop trying to go forward, maybe I can just stay here on the floor, and maybe then

I can avoid other dramatic shifts in the narrative that will only bewilder me further.

My head is propped up against the wall at an awkward angle. The broken potted plant lies tangled around my legs, the plant's roots sticking in the air like a witch's hairdo.

A large woman comes over to me and asks if I am all right. The question seems ludicrous, almost comical. But then I realize she has no idea of all the terrible things that are happening in my life at the moment, and she's just asking about the fall.

*I'm okay.*

*You sure? You look a little . . . stunned.*

*I think . . . I think I'm okay.*

*You need some help?*

I'm confused again. Can she help me with my problems, with Em, my financial situation? She's looking down at me, apprehensive now, as if she might be regretting engaging with what now seems like a crazy person.

It takes a while to register that she is asking if she can help me up.

*I'm okay.*

I've just said the same thing three times in a row. I try to get up, and she leans in to help. It's an awkward fumble with the potted plant, and she's reluctant to get too close to me and my disorientation.

Someone has righted the bench. I sit on it and try to smile and say thank you and hope I don't look or sound too crazy.

The police are leading the greasy man away in handcuffs, his baseball cap lost somewhere in the scuffle. The thin woman he was after, in a tank top with no bra, is still haranguing him, shoving her finger in his face.

*Ha, look at y'all now, you dumb, always just been a dumb junkie.*

# twenty-five

> I'll do it.

Three words. Seven letters.

Seven letters? That seems too few words for something like this. I look at the words. My thumb hovers over the *send* button.

I send it.

I stare at the screen.

Eric texts back immediately.

> Thank you Mary, you are very kind. The thought that the suffering will be over soon makes me want to break down and cry in relief. My mother and I are eternally grateful to you. I'll be in touch shortly with the next steps.

I'm at the bus stop. Someone comes and sits next to me. I put my phone away, hide it; afraid they will read what I'm about to do. My mouth is dry. I remember a juice box in my bag. I take the straw from its side and stab it in the box. Juice droplets dribble down my finger, trying to escape before I suck them down. The juice is too sweet, too concentrated. Like everything else that's happening to me, it could do with some watering down.

I notice the person next to me isn't wearing shoes. He's got plastic bags wrapped around his feet, tied with string. I try to sneak a look at the rest of him. Do I have to be afraid? I ask myself. He doesn't actually look homeless. His beard is a little shabby and his shirt is a little crumpled, but other than the shoes, he seems okay. He's writing something in a small notebook with a small pen and even smaller handwriting. Will he be able to read what he has written? I squint my eyes to see what he's writing.

*It split me in three.*

I have read enough books in my life to know what any good sentence should do. It should engage, no matter what it means. *It split me in three* is an engaging sentence. I try to get another peek at the small words on the small page.

*She has real range. From manicured princess to wide-eyed child . . . and everything in between.*

I want to see the man's face, but he's hunched over, and his curly black-and-gray hair is blocking my view. I wonder if he's a savant, like the one I read about who could count the grains of sugar in a teaspoon. Could I tell him about the dream I am living in? Would he perhaps be able to help me? He seems like a soft person; maybe it's the hair or the fact that he writes compelling words in a tiny book. Or will he turn on me, like Mad Manny did after I asked him if he would like to hear a poem I just read?

The bus hisses to a stop in front of us. The crumpled man doesn't look up from his notebook. I want to stay with him. I want to talk to him about being split in three, about Eric and his pain and Em and this strange, terrifying dream that I hope to one day wake from.

I don't want to get on the bus. I don't want to go home to my empty house and my shame that hovers above me like a nervous shadow. But I can't surrender to this madness circling me. I have to go forward, get on the bus, go home.

# twenty-six

Ms. James from the Department of Children and Families had a stern, no-nonsense manner about her. She wore a pantsuit and looked like she might have eaten a delinquent father for breakfast before she got to me. The woman sitting in my kitchen now has also been sent by the state, but she's nothing like Ms. James. This is Penny, she's twenty-four years old, and she's a social worker doing her first year of fieldwork, and I'm her first case. She has a long thin neck, a small head, and big pale-blue eyes. It looks like she might bolt at any sudden movement. She's more like an anxious deer than a person.

She also looks confused. Even a hundred layers deep in my real-time unfolding nightmare, I know why. She has read my file, and she's trying to reconcile what's in there with me, this bewildered, broken, but seemingly sweet and harmless person sitting opposite her.

She speaks in a soft and slow voice. It's punctuated with broad, sad smiles that show she's understanding of my situation. She nods almost constantly when she's listening—it's an affirming nod—although I fear if I were to mention a deep desire to cut out the entrails of stray dogs, I would be met with that same understanding nod.

She tells me of the resources provided by the state to help: food stamps, affordable health care, and continuing education. She tells me of a government program that is specifically designed to help the destitute.

The destitute—is that what I am?

She leans forward, her long neck and small face seeming almost alien.

*But more than that, I want to be here . . . for you.*

What does that mean? I wonder to myself.

*I can only imagine how difficult a time this must be for you . . . emotionally.*

I feel a rush of blood to my face. It's a sudden fear; is my plan to save my child all going to come crashing down on top of me because I can't stop myself from breaking down and confessing everything to this strange but kind woman? My face starts to crumple. Then I notice that her face is crumpling too, empathizing, mirroring me.

*I understand.*

But does she? My fear morphs into irritation. It elbows me in the ribs, eggs me on. How could she know what it's like to face the humiliation I've felt? How could she know what it's like to be contemplating shooting a man in the head?

*Life can sometimes be very difficult, but every cloud has a silver lining.*

She gives me a sad, hopeful look with those big blue eyes bulging out of her small head. What is that head full of? *Teen Vogue* "thigh gap" articles and the hopes of one day becoming a full vegan? What does she know about the slow-motion car crash that is life? Suddenly I feel the urge to leap across the table and ram my head into those disturbingly large eyes. I want to fight her, throw her against the Formica drawers. She needs to know of the madness that lurks behind every encounter, in the heart of every human. This is my act of love for her. She needs to see it. I need to beat all the shit out of her, the shit that will poison her development, stunt her potentially becoming a resilient and helpful member of society.

But I don't.

I don't fight her. I'm not a fighter. I'm like the warrior Arjuna. I don't want to fight. Instead, I just watch her and her eyes that never leave mine as she tries to remain emotionally present for me. Is this a technique she learned in a social work module?

I slump in my chair, long past exhaustion. The last fumes of the will to keep going evaporated days ago. This is just a bonus track now, dreamland stuff. I'm so utterly drained that I can barely keep breathing, but somehow I'm still moving through the world, answering the questions of twenty-four-year-old Penny from social services about the last time I felt suicidal. I want to laugh, but it's sad. I know this negative spiral has no value. *Push away, Mary, three and four, push away.*

But I'm hitting a wall. My eyes go dead as Penny blabbers on. She's taking my hand in hers now, looking at me earnestly:

*We're going to beat this. I just know it.*

I'm so tired. I start to nod off.

―――

I'm twenty layers deep in a dream within a dream when I hear knocking. It takes a long time for me to crawl up out of this heavy funk, to the surface, back to what we are calling reality. I don't know what the time is. It's dark outside. I wipe the drool from my face and check to see if Em is up. Then I see the empty bed and remember she doesn't live here anymore.

The knocking goes on. I make my way to the front door, turning the light on in the kitchen. It's Chris or Chrissy. David asked her to pick up Emma's bag. It's difficult to look at her because I know that she's sure to be looking back at me, and I know how embarrassing that must be. She's beautiful and friendly, and I'm a destitute madwoman with red welts across her face from the scrunched-up pillow she passed out on.

*If it's a bad time, I can come back. It's not a problem*, she says. (Beautiful and considerate.)

*Um, no . . . it's just . . .*

I'm still coming up from the depths of wherever I was.

*Let me . . . I'm sorry . . . Um, yes, David said something, things she needs . . .*

*It's mainly schoolbooks. The rest is not super important, I'm sure.* Chrissy helps out.

*Um, okay, yes, let me . . . Just a minute.*

I leave her at the door to contemplate my small kitchen with its fraying countertops and the stain on the floor. When I return, I hand her some books, a bag of clothes, and Em's phone charger.

I'm impressed with myself when I ask her: *Sorry, is it Chris or Chrissy?*

*Either, really, I don't mind.* She smiles. (Beautiful, considerate, easygoing.)

She says goodbye and leaves. I stand at the open door for a moment. Her presence lingers, the lightness of her beauty hovering at the border of my bleak world. It feels surreal. Was she actually here? I realize this is crazy talk. I realize that I'm still half-asleep. But I don't want to wake fully; I want to arrest my climb back up to full consciousness. I want to go back down, to where I might not be so embarrassed.

# twenty-seven

There is a letter pushed under the door when I wake up later. It's from the landlord. I've had enough letters from him over the years to recognize his handwriting. I ignore it. I have bigger things on my plate. Eric texted me. He needs to meet today. He wants to meet at Mia Bo, the coffee shop near his house.

    I shower, the hot water scalding my back, and the pain feels appropriate. I dress and put on makeup. I feel anxious, like I need to impress. Part of me realizes that I have lost perspective on how I should feel or behave. This is not a date. It's not, I know that, but I'm not casual anymore. The situation with Eric is heading down a path of no return, and some strange part of my brain says I should dress for this. I guess it's all part of the dream, and the wardrobe department suggested we dress appropriately. It's hard to look at my face in the mirror. It makes it real. The face that looks back at me is unfamiliar. I wonder if anybody would know what is going on with this person—the complexities and banalities of her life that have led to here. It's uncomfortable, so I look away.

———

The bus is empty. Just me and the driver. I wonder why. I haven't taken this route before; maybe this bus is always empty. I like the space and the silence and not having to see the suffering I usually see when I look at the faces of other people. I notice the bus driver glance in his rearview mirror at me, his lonely passenger in the back. Instantly, I'm afraid. He's a burly man. He could overpower me without breaking a sweat.

*Kind of a surprise; never had this before.* He's talking to me. His voice is light and airy and doesn't match his big body. *Just one passenger. Been driving forty-four years, don't get this. Just one passenger on a busy route. Maybe they're all out at a party we haven't been invited to.* He laughs—not the laugh you'd expect from a big man, almost a giggle. His shoulders shake.

I try to smile. Who knows what it looks like on the receiving end? I feel his need to chat. I wish I knew what to say. I don't want to displease him. I don't want him to think this is a lonely and unfriendly world, but I don't have the words. Mercifully, we come to my stop. I manage a strangled *thank you* and disappoint myself with an inability to even do that properly.

*Push away and three and four and push away.*

It's hotter than I thought as I step off the bus. The café is three blocks away, and I'm sweating by the time I arrive. Eric is there. He stands up gingerly to greet me. He looks into my eyes. It's unnerving.

*Thank you,* he says.

He seems like he might cry with gratitude. He takes my hand and gives it a little squeeze. I wonder if I will cry too. We sit.

*Would you like something to eat?*

I am acutely aware that I'm starving; well, my body is starving, but that other part of me, the nonbody part, has nearly completely detached from my physical reality, detached from the grinding flesh, and merely observes my ravenous hunger.

*Just water, thanks.*

*So I just wanted to go through the final details with you on how this will play out, if you don't mind?*

*I don't mind.*

I'm here. I'm doing this.

*This is the café you should take your Uber to. Here is the exact address.*

He hands me the business card of the restaurant. I look at it: MIA BO *Latin foods—Cuban soul.* I wonder what that means.

*You should be here at two a.m. It's open all night, so don't worry. Then you will walk to my house. It's one block up. I'll show you now, and we can walk together.*

He's looking at me, trying to gauge where I'm at, if I'm comprehending, understanding the details of this.

*But before we go, I want you to read this.* He slides a letter over to me.

To whom it may concern,

This is to confirm that I, Eric Michael Smith, Social Security number: 730-23-5980, have been suffering from acute tinnitus for several years and have come to the point that I cannot bear it anymore. I have asked Mary Williams to help me in an assisted suicide, as I am too afraid to do it myself. I am fully aware of what this entails, and I give her my permission unreservedly, absolving her of any liability for this matter in all respects.

Yours truly,
Eric Michael Smith

He's signed it in a scribble under his name.

*This will be on the kitchen table when you arrive. Take it if you feel that it might be of some help to you in any way. I don't think so, but I'm just trying to cover all the bases in case you might be worried about anything. Of course, I must ask you not to show this to anybody unless you absolutely have to, as it acknowledges that it was an assisted suicide, and as such my mother would not receive the insurance she requires to continue her medication and treatment.*

My brain just doesn't have the capacity and dexterity for the connections and decisions I need to make. I have done hours and hours of thinking over the details, and this appears to be a very simple thing that could solve seemingly impossible problems in my life. But on the other hand, I know this is a dream unfolding that I have no control over. This piece of paper might as well be a beautiful Hafiz poem describing Eric as a buffalo on the Serengeti, contemplating his existence, and it would have just as much effect on the outcome of this event. What do I know?

I make a show of trying to understand what Eric has said, but it's too complicated. It's nearly impossible to fully understand the ramifications or consequences of what I'm doing.

*Okay.* Then I add, *Thank you,* because I think that might be the right thing to say.

He gets up. He has a cane now. Did he have that before?

*Let me show you where I live.*

We walk out into the sunlight. It's harsh, and he looks very pale. We walk a block in silence.

*There . . .* He lifts his chin toward a small single-story home across the road. The garden has been maintained, the grass is bright green, and white roses line the fence. How does he get the grass so green?

*The back door will be unlocked.* We walk around the side of the house and then through the rear door into the laundry room. There is a neat stack of folded clothes on the dryer. I wonder if they will be here tomorrow when I come and shoot him . . . I push the thought away. *That's not what we're doing now. This is just a kind, sick man showing me his house,* I try to convince myself.

The kitchen has black stone counters, white cupboards, and steel appliances. It's small but immaculately clean and supremely organized. I feel my presence is contaminating the space. I ignore the voices in my head and try to focus as Eric tells me, *I'll leave the bag with your money here.* He points to a place on the floor next to the kitchen door. *Come in; walk over to the island,* he instructs me. He prompts me when I don't move.

*Please do it. It will help you tomorrow.*

I walk over to the granite island.

*Open the top drawer.*

I do as he says, and I see the black gun with a silencer lying on the striped orange oven mitts. I flinch. I've never seen a gun in real life before. It looks sinister and evil. Suddenly I want to run out of there.

Eric suddenly sits down in a chair and squeezes his eyes shut as if he is in great pain.

*Are you okay?* I ask. He starts to rub his head.

*I'm very sorry, it's just . . .* He looks frail and weak. *I just . . . Let's just try and get through this.*

I look back at the gun.

*Pick it up.*

What, me? I can't. What the hell is he thinking? Doesn't he know the kind of woman he's dealing with, the deep, inherent weakness she's made of?

*Need to . . . get used to . . .*

He struggles to get the words out. I feel bad for him. I look back down at the gun. I scurry around inside my head, frantically looking for something like courage that I might use to touch this thing. Strangely, my hand seems to be moving toward the gun. Maybe the automatic part of the dream is taking over.

I pick it up. It's cold and heavy. The silencer on the barrel weighs down the end.

*Turn . . . around.*

I do as I'm told and slowly turn to face him.

*Lift . . . it.*

I realize what he's doing, and I'm impressed by his forethought. He's easing me into this, getting me used to it. I point the gun at him.

*There are no . . . bullets . . . Pull the . . . trigger.*

My eyes widen. The pace of the dream is accelerating.

*Click.*

It sounds feeble.

*Do it again.*

What? Why?

With more force, he says, *Again!*

*Click.*

*Again.*

*Click.*

*Three times in a row.*

*Click, click, click.*

My heart is pounding, my hand shaking.

*Good.*

His approval feels comforting. A man praising me. He shakes out some pills, lifts his head slowly, and gingerly drops them into his mouth. He chews them listlessly, like he's trying to manage a great pain.

He gets to his feet slowly:

*Come.*

I follow him as he slowly walks to the bedroom. We stand under the doorway. I look around at the big bed with dark satin sheets. It feels intimate and awkward.

*Take the gun. Walk in here . . .*

He slows, but the pills seem to be working, stilling his pain.
*Come into . . . the room and fire the gun six times.*
Six times? My eyes ask him.
*I'll have taken sleeping pills, so don't worry about me.*
He looks at me. I hold my breath.
*Don't wait, don't think, Mary. Take the gun, walk in here, and pull the trigger. Both of us—we're having to override parts of ourselves to do this. It's not a normal circumstance. So don't think, don't hesitate, just do it . . . do it and then go.*

He looks at me compassionately, wearily. Life is a slow-motion car wreck, and we've both got front-row seats.

*Leave straightaway. Take the bag by the door. Then go back to Mia Bo and order an Uber.*

He takes a breath. He's getting tired.

*Take the Uber to the pier and throw the gun in the sea.*

He slows again. The pills can clearly only do so much.

*And then go on and live the life you deserve.*

We share a look. This is happening. For a brief moment I see the determination in his eyes. He wants this to happen. He is not unclear about it. I stand there on the threshold looking at his bed, the gun in my hand.

*I have to lie down now.*

I'm flustered, my perpetual anxiety: I'm a burden, not worthy of space in the world. I stumble out an apology: *Yes, yes, sorry, of course. I'll go.*

*Get some rest,* he tells me. *It'll be a long night tomorrow.*

# twenty-eight

Before I know it, the bus is spitting me out at my stop. I step off. The door hisses closed behind me, and I'm standing on the sidewalk. I don't move. An old man is trying to walk his dog on a leash, but the dog is lying down. It's like it's given up and refuses to walk anymore. I wonder how I will sleep tonight.

At home, my phone pings. It's a message from Cyril. The Try-Hards, his community theater group, are doing a small show tomorrow night. Would I like to come? He goes on to explain that he understands if it's too short notice and he doesn't want to pressure me. If I'd rather do it some other time, he fully gets it. His consideration is maddening. His deference to my judgment is exactly what I don't want. I want him to lead; I want someone who knows what the hell is going on to take charge and show me the way. I want to shelter under his surety.

I think of spending the night alone, going over what will happen at Eric's house in my head. Over and over, working through all the problems that could arise, all the risk. I'll go insane. I text him back: Thank you. That sounds nice.

He responds with: Jaya asked to come too. I should have mentioned that. I noticed the last time when I gave him a ride that you were a bit taken aback. Please forgive me for that. I should have dropped him off before I fetched you. Please don't think I'm inconsiderate.

Was I rude? I wonder if Jaya sensed that. I try to play back the last time I saw him. I remember that he sat in the back and that he was smiling. I remember his comfortable silence as he looked out the window at the passing streetlights. What was I doing? I remember anxiety, always there, like a shadow.

I'm suddenly so tired I can't think anymore. I find a can of baked beans in the cupboard. I heat them up on the stove and make some toast using stale bread I find. As the sweet smell of the beans hits my nose, I'm suddenly ravenous. I have to eat more, I remind myself. I have to be conscious about making sure I eat at least one proper meal a day to ground myself. I once read an article that stated when you don't eat, your body starts to eat itself. It eats the fat first. And then it moves on to anything else it can consume to stay alive. This cannibalism reduces the nutrition in the brain, impairs normal brain functions, and can cause hallucinations and disruptions in your heart rhythms. Is this what's happening? Is this the cause of my dream state? I bite into the toast and beans. I eat quickly, barely chewing. It feels good. I put more bread into the toaster as I start eating the second slice. The weight in my stomach feels comforting.

---

I wake up in bed with a jerk. I'm sitting upright, and everything is dark. I look at my phone. It's three in the morning. I look over at Em's bed, the geometric lines unbroken by any sleeping body lying upon it. Em is not here. Em may never be here again. I lie back down again. The silence exaggerates my predicament.

What happened? I feel the momentum building. My mind is starting to shift loose again, about to slide down into a deep, familiar pit. I feel hopeless to stop the descent, and then I remember the thing—the thing that I will do tomorrow night.

I think of the money. I stop sliding. I think of Em and the granite chessboard that I want to get her—the one we saw at the tournament here in Florida. I start climbing out of the pit . . . steady . . . one positive thought at a time, like footholds, bringing me up to the light. Determination grows in me. *Why do I have to suffer like this? Why can't I have a normal, happy life? Why Em? What has she ever done to deserve this? It isn't fair. We don't deserve this.*

*I'm going to do it.*
*That thing . . . tomorrow night.*
*I'm going to do it.*

A new feeling grows in me. Like a seedling, sped up in time, reaching for the light. I don't want to be the person I've become. I want to change. I send a text to Cyril saying: Sorry, but I can't make it. Cyril is a sweet and soft person, but I don't think I like Cyril the way he wants me to like him. I don't want him as my boyfriend. I've just never had the courage to tell him that. When faced with relentless loneliness and low self-esteem, I've gone out with him to try to feel better about myself, but I've always regretted it.

Cyril is what desperate people cling to in fear of drowning in their own pathetic situations. Cyril is not the choice a healthy Mary the Strong should make.

I don't need to go out to watch Cyril and the Try-Hards and the overly intense lead actor dominating the entire production, his thin mustache and angular face jutting out at the crowd of nine people as he berates us with his elocution. Besides, I don't have the time—I need to prepare for the reclaiming of my life.

I need to prepare for that thing I must do.

It's four in the morning. I feel different, light headed but energized. Where is this coming from? A thought pops into my head. *Go for a run.* A run in the streets at this hour? I push the hesitation aside. I haven't run for over ten years, before David and I got married. I scratch around in my closet for something to run in. Part of me shrinks when I realize how tight the clothing is, how exposed my body will be. But I push back.

I'm going to run.

---

My feet pound the ground. It's quiet out, and with each step my determination builds. With each step I'm moving away from the shame, from the helplessness. I don't want that anymore. There's no reason that Emma and I cannot have the life that everybody else has.

*Doef doef doef*

—go my feet. I feel my soul slowly being knocked back into my body with each step. I feel the sweat starting to form on my forehead, the nape of my neck. Why did I let this happen to me? Why did I just roll over and accept it like that?

*It doesn't matter, but just change now,* I answer myself in a voice that I don't recognize. Someone runs past me in the opposite direction. He looks like a wiry triathlete. His gear is high tech. He gives me a nod as he passes. I'm struck by something I have not experienced in a very long time. He's just acknowledged me as a peer. It lifts me in a way that's near intoxicating. I run harder.

*Doef doef doef*

Each step farther and farther away from the pit of pity.

*Doef doef doef*

Each step like a hammer blow, bashing me back into my body.

*Doef doef doef*

---

The early-morning sun has managed to shine through the top window of my cramped bedroom. It catches the droplets of water from the shower that bounce off my head and back. The water feels good on my tired body as I wash the sweat off. I stay in longer than I normally do, letting the water wash it away, the weakness, like a skin that has been covering me, inhibiting me. The water slowly dissolves it. It swirls around my feet and disappears down the drain.

I dry off and stand in front of the mirror naked. I need to do this. I need to own this. It's hard. There are lumps where they shouldn't be, my breasts are no longer perky, and there is no thigh gap. I force myself to look anyway, to acknowledge everything. I remember Cyril rubbing up against me, his erection straining against his pants. He wanted me. When last did I have sex? It must've been with David. I remember how he lost interest in me.

I look at my pale, naked self. I feel a tingle of desire between my legs. I run my fingers through my overgrown bush. I should shave, I think, but then I decide against it. Maybe tomorrow, after it's done.

I go to the coffee shop and order a latte and a muffin. I feel better than I have in years. What is this? For some reason I don't want to go back home. There is a growing realization in me that I have to leave there, as if the place is cursed; something slowly but surely is stifling the potential happiness of anybody who lives there. Is that why all the plants always die?

I walk along the boardwalk on a busy Sunday morning, a blue-sky day. The breeze is taking an edge off the heat, and I see many families out, kids getting balloon animals made by a clown, couples buying frozen yogurt from the pink cart. I see happy people having happy lives.

I take a seat on the bench at the end of the pier overlooking the bay. It feels good to be outside with normal people. Why haven't I done this before? Why did Em and I never just go for a walk down the pier?

I'm not going back to that life. It's over.

A fisherman and his son cast over the railing into the sea below. The lure catches the sun as it flies through the air. It glints and sparkles like a silver bird before it breaks the glass surface of the sea with a gentle *sploop!* Seagulls hover in the air just above the fisherman like a noisy halo. Their squawks are too loud. The sounds jolt me out of my reverie and back to reality.

I feel my positive mood, my determination, slowly receding, as if those loud seagulls are chasing it away. I start to feel anxious. *No, don't go.* I get up and start to move. There's a young teenage couple making out against the railing. They are trying to be discreet, but clearly they don't get much time together and want to make the most of it. They disengage and look around.

Maybe I should go for another run. I'm aware of how crazy that sounds. From no running in a decade to twice in a single day. But I'm on edge now. The dark and depressing apartment with its curse and dead plants is sucking me back, and I don't want to go. I want to stay here with the happy people. I try to smile. I try to breathe. I try to think happy thoughts. *You don't have to go back. You'll be able to get a new place for you and Em, a new place where the afternoon sun bathes the living room and the flowers bloom on the windowsill.* I feel a little better. I can do that. I will have the money to do that.

I know I can't stay here on the boardwalk forever. I have to go home and get ready. For tonight. I inhale. I know what tonight means.

*I'm not going back to that life. I'm not.* I straighten my back, inhale again deeply; I need to keep moving. This thing tonight, this may be the only chance I have to get Em back, to build a new life, to leave behind the shame, the mold, the curse.

I don't have to be there until 2:00 a.m. I have time. I don't have to go home. I could stay and have lunch here. A leisurely lunch. Isn't that what normal people do on Sundays—a leisurely lunch on the boardwalk pier?

The very thought of this is outrageous. When last did I eat out at a restaurant, an expensive pier-side restaurant? I stand on the boardwalk as people drift past me in both directions. I'm on some kind of precipice. I can go home to the dark, tearstained apartment, or I can stay here with these people bathed by the sun of good fortune.

I stand there.

I watch a mother and her daughter walk past. The young daughter just said something, and the mother has her head thrown back, laughing. The daughter smiles at her own wit, and she tells her mother, *And they think that will work on me, fat chance*! It's extraordinary: the lightness of their relationship, the confidence of the young girl. They walk into *Pierre's on the Pier*. The maître d' hands them a menu and welcomes them.

I turn and walk toward *Pierre's on the Pier*.

# twenty-nine

It's dusk when I wake up. My head is thick from the sun and the wine I had at lunch. I must've dozed off on the couch. I swing my feet to the floor and look around.

The tap is dripping into the sink. *Drip, drip, drip, drip.* I feel the familiar tentacles of desperation and sadness creeping toward me, creeping out from the corner of the room, making their way over to me. I hate this place.

I get up and walk over to the sink and turn off the faucet. I look at the clock on the wall. Six hours to go. I drink a glass of water. It tastes like chlorine and poverty. I don't know how I will be able to sit here for the next six hours. Maybe I could go out, to a bar or something. But then I think about all the crowds and the noise and the intimidating young people. Cyril? I could call Cyril and go to the performance. No, I tell myself. I can't go backward, not anymore.

I turn on the TV. It's some reality show with people on an island. The host is explaining the changes to the challenge for the five remaining contestants. There's something wrong with the host's face . . . too tanned, his skin too stretched.

He's wearing one of those shirts with little loops of rope on the pockets and sleeves. The contestants look thin and healthy. There's a young woman whose eyes are as blue and clear as the sea behind her.

The host drops his arm, and the remaining contestants gallop into the shadows of the sea before diving into the water and swimming after one of five buoys. My legs start to bounce. I don't think I'm going to be able to just sit here until it's time to leave.

My mind starts to drift. I picture Eric's kitchen, going to the drawer, walking over the threshold of his bedroom, *click, click, click*. I think of the bag by the door. Do I count the money? No, definitely not. Do I look inside . . . maybe? I start to feel nervous, butterflies in my stomach. What if I can't do it? I try to visualize it again, walking inside, seeing the bag by the door. I don't open it. I go to the drawer, take out the gun, and walk into— *You lied! We were in an alliance, and you straight-up lied in my face!* The pretty blue-eyed girl on the TV is angry, shouting at an older woman. The older woman looks genuinely sorry. Her face is crinkled and dark from the sun. She's stumbling over her words of apology, clearly under tremendous stress.

*I didn't—it wasn't like that. I said I was voting for you, but I was just agreeing with him when he said you were the biggest threat left. But I didn't—I wasn't planning to vote for you, I'm sorry, really, I'm sorry, I . . .* She's crying now, emotionally exhausted by the freak show they call reality TV. I look at the clock. Five hours and forty-eight minutes to go.

———

The hours pass agonizingly slowly. It feels like a level of hell. I'm panicking. I'm struggling to stop my hands from shaking, imagining everything that could go wrong. I can't push away the bad thoughts. They all come for me, clawing at me like grieving relatives, wanting my attention.

All the while, the host is snuffing out torches and people are leaving the island. And then there were six and then five, then four, and finally three. I can't sit still. I shower three times, trying to drown out the relentless barrage of questions. *What if you can't do it? What if you miss? What if he's awake? What if he changes his mind? What if the gun jams?*

But somehow, the hours pass and now it's 1:50 a.m., and I'm in the back seat of an Uber. My phone says we are three minutes away.

The driver is silent—tired, I imagine, from a long shift, tired from the effort to keep poverty away. I understand. I too have to do difficult things to keep poverty away. I have to raise a gun and shoot a man in the he— *Stop thinking. Do. Act! For once in your life, stop being so passive. Do this. Take control of your life.* I have to keep this pep talk going constantly, or I will be swallowed by panic. Both sides fight for their right to be heard.

*You can't kill a person. That's murder, no matter what anybody says. You can't take a gun and shoot someone. That's crazy.*

*No, it's not. It's kindness. There are assisted suicides every day of every week of every year, and this act helps not only a suffering man but his sick mother too. This is what people do in the world. This is the mess of life that I cannot avoid anymore. If I want harmony, I have to create it. It doesn't instantly appear like I thought it would.*

*You're insane. This is what crazy people do. Go home and call Penny, the social worker. She has been specifically assigned to help you. That's their job, to help people get back on their feet.*

*You mean the same people who took away Emma?*

Back and forth, back and forth it goes, no side willing to take a breath, fearing the other side's dominance. My legs are bouncing in the back seat; I'm picking at my nails; the minutes are counting down. I feel like a bird in a cage surrounded by dozens of starving cats. I flit from one perch to the next, trying to keep them all in my line of sight.

The Uber pulls up outside Mia Bo.

*We're here,* he says as he leans forward and punches something into the phone mounted on the dash.

I thank him and close the door behind me as he drives off. I start walking quickly toward Eric's house. I fear that if I stop even for a second, I won't be able to go through with it. Then I remember Eric's instruction was to go into the café. I start to walk back toward Mia Bo. It's dark, and no one is around. I see the warmth of life inside the café. A big man sits in a booth hunched over his phone. That's when I realize that I was meant to go into the café *after* the deed was done, not before.

Shit! I start to panic. I look at my watch—it's 2:01. I'm shaking, and I can feel my heart pounding in my chest like it will break through my ribs.

———

I see Eric's house. There are no lights on. I want to burst into tears, my anxiety is so acute. My whole body is shaking. A car drives past, and I freeze. It's the police—I know it more than I've ever known anything. The car passes, disappearing into the darkness up the street. It isn't the police. A dull wash of moonlight picks up the white roses that line the garden fence. They look strange in the blue-gray light of the night. I'm nearly running. I have to slow down. Adrenaline is pulsing through my body like someone has forgotten to tell it to stop. My whole body is tingling.

I walk/run down the side of the house, around to the back door. I stop. I pray it's locked. I can't do this. I try the door, and it opens without any noise. I see the neat stack of folded laundry on the dryer. The door from the laundry room to the kitchen is open. There is a low light on a dimmer in the living room. I see the bag at the door. It looks full.

The house is quiet. I don't know how, but as if pushed by some resilience I didn't know I had, I'm walking inside the house, into the kitchen. I'm hyperaware—the adrenaline has made me so. The kitchen is spotless. I see myself walking over to the kitchen drawer. Eric was right; the rehearsal has made this easier. I know what to expect, but when I see the gun, it still shocks me—the shiny black color, the silencer, like in the movies, like assassins use. I wonder how I am doing this as I see my hand reaching for the gun. I feel the cold, heavy metal. My breathing seems slower, or maybe I'm not breathing. My heart palpitates like I'm about to have a heart attack. There's a note above the drawer: *Thank you, Mary, may God bless you. All my love, Eric.* It's a good note because I'm turning my body, my feet are moving forward, and I'm moving toward the door of the bedroom. My brain is spinning, my heart exploding, my sight blurry from all the static noise in my head, but I'm doing it. I'm watching myself doing it. I'm coming to the doorway. I see his shape under the sheet, and I raise the gun.

*PHHHHT*

*PHHHHT*

*PHHHHT*

*PHHHHT*

The pillow is exploding with feathers. There is a pink mist coating the wall.

*PHHHHT*

*PHHHHT*

I see his body bouncing.

*Click*

*Click*

*Click*

I'm vaguely aware there are no more bullets.

I stop.

Eric's body slowly rolls off the bed and crumples to the floor. I stand there with a gun at my side, the strange smell of cordite filling the air, a wisp of smoke escaping from the nose of the silencer.

I look at Eric lying on the floor, the glazed eyes. He looks different. My brain is trying to do the math, put together the pieces, but it can't. Something is wrong.

I look harder, and then I realize what my brain is struggling to figure out.

The person lying dead on the bedroom floor is not Eric Smith.

# PART II

*Everyone has a plan until they get punched in the face.*
—Mike Tyson

# thirty

I'm running into the black night. I fall. The skin on my palms and knees grinds into the hard asphalt. My lungs burn. I might be screaming, but I can't be sure. I crash into a pile of metal trash cans, tumble over a bin. My hands stick into something wet and glutinous as I push myself back onto my feet. I run and run and run.

———

A key verse in the Bhagavad Gita, the Vedic text about Krishna and the reluctant warrior Arjuna, says the soul is eternal and cannot be destroyed even when the body is destroyed. The Sanskrit is *na hanyate—indestructible*. When I read that, I felt safe, like no matter what happened on the outside, inside I would always remain whole, regardless.

But standing inside the bedroom of what I thought was Eric Smith's house and seeing on the floor the dead body of a person I'd never met before, I felt something break. Something deep inside me. I felt my soul, that eternal, indestructible force, crack. Seeing the pool of blood around the man's head, I realized I was facing a stark reality, the harshest, most brutal and unburnished version of existence. It was horrifying. It was death. It was murder. I don't think anyone should ever see something so empty of grace, so godless. And to think it was I who had just done this—well, the reality was too sharp, and that eternal part of me broke.

My brain was moving too fast, desperately trying to find a way to comprehend what my senses were processing. My eyes were seeing the blood, my nose smelling the cordite, my ears hearing my gasp.

This was murder.

A reality my mind, understandably, could not accept. My mind was frantically searching for an alternate conclusion, any conclusion.

Just not this. Not the dead man on the floor.

I stumbled backward out of the bedroom, my back knocking into the granite counter behind me, the hard slab of stone smacking into my lower spine.

I turned. The bag was gone, or was the bag never there? I started to run.

And run

    and run

        and run

            and run

                and run.

---

My lungs are on fire. What happened? Did I go to the wrong house? A car backs out of a driveway and almost hits me. He jams on the brakes at the last moment. As he sees me, his brow furrows with confusion, noticing I'm not an early-morning jogger but a middle-aged woman with blood drying on her knees and madness in her eyes as she runs and cries.

He unbuckles his seat belt and gets out of his car.

*Hey!*

I quickly turn to see him standing behind his car, a barrier between himself and whatever I might be. I keep running. Then I remember the gun in my bag. I have to get to the pier. I have to get rid of the gun. The gun! My God, it's real. I shot a person in the head. He's dead.

Panic and fear fight desperately over my soul, each sure of its rightful claim. Where am I? I've been running blindly. You can't get to the pier unless you know where you are. I look around as I run—just suburban houses on a suburban street. In the distance, I see two cars cross each other on the street. It's the main road. I slow to a walk. I swallow. Reality up ahead. People. My hands throb. I look at the dark blood and the grazed skin on my palms. I look down at my knees. Blood stains the left knee. I spit on my good hand and try to rub away the blood. The skin is raw and painful, but I don't care. I get closer to the main street. I see the coffee shop that makes the fresh muffins. I know where I am. I quickly cross into the safe darkness of the neighborhood on the other side of the main street.

I start running again. It's impossible to just walk calmly. A dog barks loudly at a gate as I go past. My heart shatters, and I almost fall over from fright. I'm brittle, too brittle, as if I'm an inch away from annihilation. I don't stop; I keep running. I have to get rid of the gun. I tire suddenly, immediately. I can't run anymore. The adrenaline is wearing off, and my knee and palms are hurting unbearably. I think I might pass out from exhaustion, but then I smell the salt in the air. The beach, it's close. I round the corner and see the Ferris wheel in the distance. The pier!

I push myself to keep going. The sound of my feet hitting the wood of the pier is music to my ears. The weather-beaten planks buckle and rattle with each step. The shops and restaurants in the center of the boardwalk are all closed. I see a man walking his little white poodle on the beach. He's looking in the other direction and doesn't see me. I swerve to the other side of the T-shirt shop to block his vision in case he turns this way.

And then I hear them.

People laughing. Men or boys. Fear squeezes hard at my heart. I almost knock into a couple making out under the awning of the T-shirt shop. And then I see the others, on their haunches, smoking, drinking: six, eight of them, men/boys. A gold chain glints under an overhead light. I'm frozen. They look at me. I look back, like a helpless lamb. I turn around and start walking back, clasping my bag to my chest. I can feel my heart pounding. How much more of this can I take? I'm waiting for a hand on my shoulder to pull at me, a voice to call me back, footsteps to come after me. I hear a male voice and then laughter exploding out of their group. I know that sound. I'm a joke to them. Hot tears come again, and I'm running back down the pier toward the beach. I can't keep this up. The man with his dog is farther down the beach. As I reach the end of the pier, I turn in the opposite direction. The sand is heavy and wet. I can't lift my feet; it's like running in cement, but I have to get away from the lights of the pier, into the darkness of the beach. The waves crash to my left. I look back, but no one is following me. I keep running.

Beachfront houses stick out from behind the sand dunes. I run over a dune and see a field mouse scramble under a bush. I fall. The sand is hard and granular now. It scratches my face. I crawl over the small dune, down into the firepit area of an empty cottage. I can't stay here; this is someone's house. I have to keep moving, but my legs won't function. There's nothing left. I'll rest a minute and then go on. Just for a moment. I need to keep moving. Just a minute . . . can't stay . . . must keep . . .

# thirty-one

He hears her come in. He can't fucking believe it! She came! His heart starts to beat so loudly that he wonders if she might be able to hear it. He's leaning against the wall in the darkness of the living room. Then he sees her. *She's going for the drawer! My God, she's actually doing it!*

She takes the gun and starts to walk toward Mark's bedroom. Seeing how quiet she is, Eric realizes he didn't need to slip Mark that sedative earlier. There was no way he would have heard her. Now it's going to come up in a blood test, and that may require some answers.

Still, it wasn't something you could just risk. How the hell was he meant to know? It wasn't like he had planned a murder before.

Eric watches her enter the bedroom, and then he quietly ducks into the kitchen, picking up the bag at the door. He hears the first shot muffled by the silencer. And then another and another. He slips back into the darkness of the living room.

He hears the thump of Mark falling out of the bed and a moment of silence before her gasp of shock. He waits. And then she's gone, bashing open the laundry room door and running like a madwoman down the street.

He waits for another few seconds.

He can't believe it.

She did it.

He walks forward to stand at the threshold of Mark's bedroom. Mark is dead, his legs still on the bed, tangled under the sheets, and his head and body on the floor. Blood makes a red crown around his head on the carpet. A bullet seems to have shot off half his left ear. There're two bullet holes in his chest as well. It looks ugly and messy, not at all like he imagined.

Eric walks into the room and sits on the edge of the bed and takes out his phone. He takes a moment, inhales. His expression starts to change. He swallows, blinks his eyes, as if preparing for something. He dials the number:

*911, what is your emergency?*

*My—my boyfriend's been shot.*

———

The red and blue lights from the police cars wash over the neighboring houses. They're parked outside Mark's house. An old couple are standing on the porch looking over the road at the quaint house with the well-cared-for green grass and white roses. They look concerned and frightened.

A body is rolled out of the house on a gurney. The medics lift the bed and roll it in one motion into the open belly of the ambulance. Inside the house, police swarm. There must be a dozen people inside. There's police tape, clipboards, furrowed brows, blue-gloved hands with little brushes and evidence bags.

In the living room, Eric is sitting on the edge of the sofa. A detective sits opposite him. Eric is giving his full name: Eric Andrew Wilson. Not Eric Smith, as he told Mary. He couldn't very well have told her his real name. Eric looks ashen and shocked. He's practiced this look, studied it. He watched movies with Mark on this very sofa, studying the actors, mostly women—Amy Adams, Natalie Portman, Rosamund Pike—who do this shocked, devastated look, with its slow creep toward grief. Sometimes he even rewinds the movie to a particularly relevant scene, noting the reddening of the face, the tears. Mark didn't know what he was doing. Eric was a mystery to Mark; he found Eric mysterious and alluring. Eric hated that Mark was so dumb.

The young officer is asking Eric another question.

*I'm sorry, it's just . . .* Eric brings his hands up to his face, swallows back tears as his fingers tremble slightly. He watched Nicole Kidman do this exact thing in a scene from *Rabbit Hole* after her character's son died from cancer. It was so good. Eric remembers to roll his fingers into a fist in front of his eyes for a moment and slowly tap his fist against his face, just as she did.

*Take your time, Mr. Wilson, take your time,* says Officer Lewis.

*Maybe I should get into acting,* Eric thinks. The officer is a young guy with a strange, pinched face and a neat crop of hair. He doesn't really look like a cop, Eric thinks. He would have preferred a more handsome, more photogenic face to be interviewing him.

Officer Lewis is asking Eric whether he has seen any strangers in the neighborhood recently, anyone suspicious he hasn't seen before. The officer mentions a gang working in the area whose members wear red-and-white bandannas.

*Have you seen anyone like that recently? They're mostly Hispanic.*

Eric looks at the young officer, seeing his lack of presence and authority, like he's unsure whether this is the right question to be asking. Eric is disappointed. He was expecting some more confidence here. This all lacks the dramatic tension he imagined.

*No . . . I don't think so . . .*

# thirty-two

I feel heat on my face and hear a noise I can't identify, like a muffled grunt. And the smell . . . Shit? Booze? I feel rough hands on the tender skin of my breast. I'm confused. I have to make my way back to consciousness, but I feel so tired. I just want to sleep. I roll onto my side.

---

I doze off. I don't know for how long.

A dog barks and I wake up with a start.

I look around. I'm on the porch at the back of the beach house. The window frames are rusted from the salty sea air. No one has been here for a while. The sand and wind have formed miniature sand dunes at the far end of the porch. The sun beats down on me. I get to my feet. My knees hurt as the skin tears again. I catch a glimpse of myself in the murky reflection of the window. I look like a homeless person. There's sand in my hair. My eyes are puffy and red. My dress has a stain on the left shoulder.

I remember his face, the man's face, the man I shot.

The gun! It's still in my bag! The fear storms me, but my body is too tired, my adrenal glands too depleted, to turn the emotion into action. But I know I have to act. I must get rid of the gun.

I walk up a little on the sand dune and look over the beach and the pier. There are people everywhere. Beachgoers are setting up their umbrellas. Shops on the boardwalks are open. Tourists are browsing. I walk back down to the beach house. I see one of the wooden vertical slats has fallen out of the railing of the porch. I notice a gap under the porch floor. I stumble over and start digging. I dig and I dig.

The sand becomes colder and thicker. It's hard going. I look around, wondering if somebody will see me. I dig more until the hole is about two feet deep. I look around again, but I'm out of sight, obscured by the dunes. I take the gun and drop it into the hole. It falls with a meek thud. I fill the hole back up, using my arms to sweep the piles of sand back into the hole.

I hear a dog bark again somewhere. What if the dog digs it up? I should find another place. My fingerprints! Dammit, my fingerprints are all over the gun! I have to dig it up. The barking dog is getting closer. I can't stay here; someone is coming. I get back to my feet, and the salt in the sand stings the cut on my knees. I walk around the side of the house and cross onto the neighbor's property. They have an outside staircase leading up to a second-floor balcony. I duck under the staircase. And wait.

The dog's barking fades away, its owner leading it in the other direction. I need to get home. I can't stay out in public looking like this any longer. I try to find a bus schedule on my phone. It's eight minutes to noon. What day is it, Monday? The next bus is in an hour. I'll have to wait. Then I realize I don't have any money. I have to order an Uber. I can't keep hiding like this.

I punch my address into the Uber app. The Uber Pool is

thirty-three dollars. UberX is forty-eight. I can't pool, not looking like this. Do I even have forty-eight dollars on my credit card? I don't care; I have to get home. I confirm the UberX. But it doesn't go through. My credit card is declined.

I bite my lip. I want to cry again; no, I want to die. I picture the police arresting me, dragging me out from underneath the staircase. I see a faucet at the side of the house. Coming out from under the staircase, I look around. The houses all seem empty. I go over to the tap and turn it on. Water belches out, brown and warm. I wash my face; it wakes me up. I drink, gulping down the water. My throat gags. I get as much water as I can into my body and wash the blood off my knees and palms. I try to shake the sand from my hair. I drink some more water, and it rolls around in my empty stomach as I stand up. I feel I might be sick.

I'm going to have to walk home. I poke my head around the side of the house and look out toward the road. In the distance, I can see a woman putting something into the back of her car. It's a small Japanese car, and the trunk closes with a thin clunk. The car looks too small, unsafe. I worry for her, thinking that she might get into a car accident. I can see the thin, crumpled metal colliding with her frail body. She drives off. I feel the sun hot on my head. I start walking, trying not to look like a murderer.

# thirty-three

Six months ago, Detective Fennella Rose considered for the first time in her twenty-three-year career that maybe this wasn't the job for her, that maybe she should resign and start a flower shop and begin painting watercolors like she had always thought about.

She was standing in the courtroom. Judge Landon's courtroom. A courtroom that was always a mess of papers and lateness and old broken benches. Rose hated this courtroom. Landon had just banged his gavel and, without even looking around, declared a mistrial. The evidence against the confessed murderer of a young jogger was vast and conclusive. But somewhere along the way, his DNA sample had been contaminated, and now despite his confession, he was free to go. His name was Nicky Valdez. Detective Rose had arrested him. He had spit in her face and called her an ugly bitch. He had said that he was going to rape her too when he got the chance. Now Valdez was walking out of the courtroom a free man. He smirked at Detective Rose as he walked past.

She sat in the empty courtroom for nearly two hours after that, wondering about her future as a policewoman, wondering about that smirk on his face, and wondering about the dead jogger, who had first been beaten and raped.

Mostly, Rose wondered about justice and whether there was an inherent order in the world. She asked herself how people like Nicky Valdez could walk free. She wondered about killing him herself. She was not a violent person. In fact, she abhorred violence and the damage it could do to the skin and bones of innocent people. Nevertheless, she was so shocked that such a person could go unpunished she considered that perhaps she was duty bound to right this wrong. Surely to allow such injustice was in itself a crime.

Her superior and mentor, Captain Dietricks, had once given her a glass plaque embossed with the words *The only thing necessary for the triumph of evil is for good men to do nothing.* It had struck her deeply. It was a code that had guided her, those words often pushing her to work later and harder than she otherwise would have. It was an obligation she felt in her bones, and for that she was prepared to sacrifice her sleep, her weekends, her hobbies.

She knew that she was a good person, just as she knew that there were evil people. Nicky Valdez was clearly one of those, so what should she do? She understood there was a part of her that could take the emotion out of it and pull the trigger, right the wrong. But was this really what was required of her?

She never managed to answer the question that day. Later that week, when she told her sister that she was thinking of leaving the force, her sister's young daughter asked who would protect her then. Hearing that, Rose decided to hold off leaving for the near future. Still, something has not been right with her since. Now she sees a blurry area that was once a clearly defined black and white.

The days have drifted into weeks and the weeks into months,

and this unease has become a distant memory, until she walks into the Mark Matthews crime scene and sees the smirk on Eric Wilson's face. She knows that smirk. She saw it before on the face of Nicky Valdez, and with that smirk, all those emotions rush right back into her.

# thirty-four

Eric thinks that Detective Rose looks more the part. She's not pretty at all, but Eric can see she clearly knows what she's doing. She has authority. Eric likes that. That's her job: the no-nonsense detective on a murder case. She sits down in front of Eric. Eric notices the pair of gray Crocs she's wearing. He wants to smirk at her again, smirk at her blatant rebellion against anything beautiful, but he restrains himself, remembering that he has a part to play here.

She looks at him with her flat, ugly face. Eric isn't intimidated. He prepared for her. He prepared for everything. He knows they have nothing.

Detective Rose asks Eric if he wouldn't mind coming down to the station with them. It would be easier, she says. They need to finish up a few questions and get a DNA swab. *Just to make sure when we sweep the place, we know what isn't yours and Mark's.*

Eric knows he doesn't have to go. He knows that his relationship with Detective Rose is going to deteriorate very quickly. He knows that there's no way he isn't the prime suspect here. It's always the lover. But also he knows: They don't have anything. And they never will. He has thought this all through . . . all of it.

So going won't be a problem, but why not add a little resistance here, see how the hardworking, no-nonsense detective reacts?

*Can we do this in the morning? I really don't* . . . He pauses, gathers himself, like he saw Julianne Moore do in *Still Alice*. She went on to win the Academy Award for her performance.

*I need to rest.*

*It won't take a minute, Mr. Wilson. It'll be in and out.*

He looks at her through his red and tired eyes.

*I'm sorry, I'm very tired. I just don't have it in me right now.*

*This place is going to be a railway station for the next twelve hours with people coming and going. You won't get any rest here.*

*It's okay. I'll go back to my apartment.*

Rose considers him. She's been doing this for over twenty-three years. This is her eighty-ninth homicide. Looking at Eric Wilson and his dramatic performance as the grieving boyfriend, she knows that Eric Wilson is guilty.

She's as sure as she's ever been that he killed his boyfriend.

But she also knows how many guilty men have walked free before. She wants him without his lawyer. If she pushes too hard now, she may lose her best chance at that. She doesn't want another Nicky Valdez. There will be no mistrial here, she tells herself. This is the last time some guilty bastard smirks at her.

She softens, puts on her own performance now.

*No, of course. I just thought it would be easier for you, but it's okay. You rest up. Let's do it a little later. Try and get some sleep, and I'll send a car over later.*

---

Eric is nodding. He doesn't like her, he decides. *She thinks I'm a child.* Fuck her and her ugly face and her thick ankles.

*Okay, thank you,* he says.

She stands and says to Officer Lewis, *Help him with anything he needs.*

Eric has his head in his hands as he stares at the floor. He doesn't see Detective Rose gesturing for Lewis to follow her.

*Keep an eye on him*, she says to Lewis under her breath.

# thirty-five

There is a piece of paper stuck on my apartment door. It's the state of Florida explaining that my nonresponse to the writ of restitution has resulted in me being evicted from my apartment. I have to read the notice several times to understand it. I am delirious from walking six miles in the heat. My adrenals are depleted. I try my key several times, but it can't unlock my door. They've changed the locks. I slide down and crumple onto the old doormat, completely depleted.

Who was I to think I had reached the bottom of my pain? *You, dear Mary, clearly still have a long way to go.* It seems that I have yet to experience a depth of hell that I never even knew existed. Maybe this is just the beginning. Maybe the day I was punched in the face by my husband is a time I'll look back upon fondly. At least I had a daughter then. And a house and food to eat. I should kill myself. I think of the gun in the sand under the house with the rusty window. I should kill myself, but I can't get up.

*I saw you*
*and you saw nothing,*
*kept talking*

*to the empty walls.*
*Am I a ghost,*
*a dream?*
*Please, dear God,*
*can I be a dream*
*and this hellish world*
*not be real?*

*And this hellish world not be real.* The words swim in my head. *Please, please, can I, can this, not be real.*

My hand aches. I see the torn skin on my palm. Real pain on a real body. Real. No dreams for the wicked. The wicked killer of innocent men.

Who is he? That man I shot. What is going to happen to me? Am I going to jail for the rest of my life? Am I a murderer?

I hear a noise. I don't register it at first. Is it a noise from this world or my dreamworld? I know that both have the capacity to kill me. I can die and suffer just as acutely in the dreamworld as I can in the real world. It's just good to know which place I'm in. The rules might be different, but maybe not. I don't know the rules in either world anyway. In whatever world I am currently living in, it seems as though the rules are changing all the time. How can my life have all the hallmarks of a normal life and yet still be so hellishly otherworldly?

I realize the noise is an incoming message on my phone. It must be the real world. I contemplate going through my bag. But what good will it do to look at a message on my phone? No few letters on a phone screen are going to save a woman as doomed as I. Lying there, I groan in dull agony.

The phone buzzes again. I feel around like a drunk in my bag. My fingers clasp the phone's edge. I bring it up to my face.

> Thinking of you. Hope all is well. Cyril. ☺

My lips tremble. Cyril, sweet Cyril. His kind message devastates me, and I convulse in tears and snot.

———

I'm sitting on the sidewalk when his car pulls up. By the look on his face, I can tell that he is shocked by the extreme state I'm in. He came as fast as he could. I feel a rush of gratitude for kind people like him. I feel unworthy of his kindness. He pulls over, one front wheel knocking against the curb in his haste, then leaps out and runs over to me. I don't have the energy to get up. When he gets a closer look at the wreck of me, his mouth forms an O. He hesitates, not sure if he can follow through, pick me up in his arms, and save me. I have no way to tell him anything. I am a shell, the outside of a person who has had her insides cut away with a blunt knife. After a period of time that seems to span eternity, he finally reaches down and pulls me to my feet, then embraces me. I melt into tears again. I can feel his apprehension at how horrifically broken I am. But he continues to hold me as I soak his shoulder in tears.

Mary the Strong, now Mary the Broken. Do people know how easily this can happen, even to the most resilient? A layoff, a difficult divorce, a health setback—how quickly a steady, ordinary life can turn for the worse.

Eventually Cyril breaks the embrace. He holds me at arm's length, his face swimming in concern and confusion: *What happened?*

I couldn't say anything even if I wanted to. I don't know how words work anymore—their meanings, pronunciations. I'm about to break down again. Then, mercifully, he simply says: *Come, let's go.*

# thirty-six

Eric rubs the moisturizer on his skin with his outstretched index fingers. One for each cheek, concentric circles, slowly, slowly. He dabs a dollop on his forehead and one on his chin and then rubs in the cream. It was a late night. He hasn't had much sleep, and he looks terrible. It plays well for what he is supposed to be feeling, but he just can't face going outside without at least some moisturizer. He has to resist putting on some base to cover up the black smudges under his eyes. He thinks of Mark, who could go out after an all-nighter and still have the glow of a nubile youth.

He resents that everything he's ever gotten has only been the product of hard work and conscientious planning. Why does it all entail such labor? It makes him jealous of those to whom it comes easy. Like Mark. It isn't fair.

How many months of planning and plotting and researching did it take so there would be no trail back to Eric when the detectives came looking? And he knew without a doubt they would come looking. All for what? Around half a million, after estate fees and whatever other hidden costs are surely going to crop up. He wishes he had taken out the premium package with the larger insurance payout, the $10 million option. But the whole business got so complicated. He had to first convince Mark to buy a policy, and then he had to make sure that he was the primary beneficiary without raising any suspicion. He went as far as staging a dramatic "accident" while jogging.

Eric came home with a cut on his elbow, regaled Mark with a story that a car had come out of nowhere and almost killed him. He told Mark he had thought it was over and that all he could think about was him. He said that they had to be more careful; this world was a dangerous place, and they should do whatever they could to protect each other. It was dramatic and emotional. Mark was taken aback by Eric's sudden sentiment, but he welcomed it. Mark lived for this kind of melodrama. Eric struggled to keep up the act. He waited a full twenty-four hours before he suggested the idea of life insurance. *We should do it together, matching life insurance policies,* he suggested. *It'll be romantic.*

Mark fell for it, of course. But all the paperwork, the details, and the decisions about the premiums—higher payout equaled higher premiums—sucked all the passion out of it for Mark, and Eric became impatient and irritable. The problem was that Eric didn't know how long he would have to pay the premiums, how long it would take him to find a "Mary," some desperate and crazy person who'd actually agree to do something as radical as he needed.

He and Mark eventually settled on the million-dollar policy. The whole thing became an ordeal, and after they signed the documents, they barely spoke to each other for days afterward. Pushing for the $10 million premium package was just not an option. Of course, having taken out a life insurance policy on his lover just months before his murder will place all the suspicion on him. Eric knows that. He is ready for that and isn't concerned. He has planned this all meticulously, and he knows the police have nothing and will find nothing. He will just have to ride out the suspicion and all their scratching around. *Fuck them* is the two-word mantra that Eric will use to get through all of it. *Fuck the broad-faced cop, fuck the newspapers, fuck the lawyers, fuck the salacious details. Fuck everyone. You ain't got nothing.*

Eric closes the lid of his expensive moisturizer and places it back in his neatly arranged row of equally expensive toiletries. They are an indulgence, but Eric decided a long time ago that it was worth it. Quality grooming products are an investment in the valuable commodity that is his appearance.

He looks back into the mirror and reluctantly accepts that the dark rings are indeed the perfect accessory for a grieving spouse. He knew that Detective Rose wouldn't buy it, his grieving spouse act, but what was he meant to do? Tell her to "catch me if you can"? That was what he'd wanted to do, and that's pretty much what this all amounts to. Try to catch him. Any detective worth anything would see him as the primary suspect immediately. But suspicion isn't enough, and Eric has been careful to make sure that that's all they're ever going to have. Still, it would be odd not to at least try to put on a pretense of innocence. It'll be like a game, the things said by him, the things said by her, neither actually saying the things they know to be true.

He knows who Detective Rose is, at least theoretically. Eric did his homework on which detective might walk through the door of Mark's house that night, given who has jurisdiction in that area. He feared Detective Rose the most. Not just because she seems like the least glamorous person in the history of humanity, and nothing sours Eric's mood more than people who see no value in beauty and style. They're the real psychopaths of the world, Eric thinks. No, the biggest threat that Detective Rose poses is that her astounding lack of personality has given her a machinelike determination to do her job with the regularity and efficiency of a robot. She doesn't tire or become emotional or discouraged, just like she never becomes excited or hopeful.

She simply does her job until it's done. Rain or snow, mountains of evidence or no evidence, cooperative witnesses or defiant ones, she doggedly goes about her work until the bad people are behind bars. And then she goes home and makes a different meal for each day of the week, as she has been doing for the last decade, watches a little TV—wildlife documentaries, mainly—and then goes to bed after reading a few verses from her King James Bible. Eric hates her and everything she stands for. He looks forward to fucking with her.

# thirty-seven

The police station is as drab and thoughtless as he expected. *I guess everybody has to play their part*, he surmises. The whole thing is like a cheap movie set that had no real money for art direction or authentic props. The table is Formica, and the chairs are from Lowe's. They called it the interview room, but Eric knows that it is in fact an interrogation room. They're going to try to interrogate him. Eric has thought about getting a lawyer but ultimately decided against it because of the cost. He knows that if for some unexpected reason things go awry, he'll have no choice but to hire one. For now, however, he knows they have nothing.

Detective Rose walks in and tries a smile. It's stiff and alien. *I'll bet she hates this part*, Eric thinks, *trying to be nice.*

*Thank you for coming in. We understand it's not the best time for you.*

He looks at her sadly through his red-rimmed eyes. She holds the look a bit longer than most people would. She's trying to read him, he thinks, but it's pretty clear she's convinced that he killed his lover.

*This is really just protocol . . . get the paperwork out of the way.*

She slides a tape recorder across the desk.

*You don't mind, do you? It's going to save everybody asking you the same thing a hundred times.*

Eric knew this was coming: he has to formally proclaim his innocence for the record, and there's no getting around that. He could just say no, but that would risk them pushing hard to try to get an arrest warrant. They don't have anything, and you can't just get a warrant on suspicion, but it is a risk he isn't prepared to take.

*No, not a problem. Just let me know how I can help.*

She wants him to recall the evening, so he does: the dinner, the wine (he leaves out the part where he slipped the sleeping pills into Mark's dal curry), TV (*House of Cards*, the final season with just Robin Wright), and then bed.

*And then I heard something that woke me up . . .*

He remembers to break down during this part, take his time to recover . . . take longer than the good detective would like before he gets back to the story. He tries to get her to push him, test her patience with his "grief." He wants to make her seem rude and insensitive to his recent tragedy.

*So you don't remember exactly what the sound was that woke you?*

He starts to answer, remembering to always add the caveats: the *can't be sures*, the *hard to tells*, the *I think sos*, the *maybes*, nothing definitive, nothing solid. He breaks down regularly, apologizes, asks for water, takes a moment to gather himself. He sets the rhythm, not her. He knows she hates this. He doesn't give a shit because he knows . . .

. . . they have nothing.

*Maybe a bang . . . or maybe . . . I don't know, something. I heard something . . . and then I woke up.*

*And you saw the victim.*

*Yes.*

She looks at him. She tries to hide it, the *aha* moment pinging so loudly in her head, but Eric sees it, adjusts. *I think so. I can't be so sure . . .*

She frowns, almost imperceptibly.

*I, I . . . the blood . . .*

He wells up with emotion, digs deep for tears. *When in doubt start to cry* has been a great strategy so far.

*If we could get back to when you woke up. You said you heard a bang, like a gunshot?*

Eric reminds himself not to answer straightaway.

*I'm sorry, it's just . . .* He rubs his eyes.

*And then you saw him, Mark, your boyfriend, and the blood.*

He waits.

*What is she going for here?* he wonders. It's something, for sure, but he doesn't know what. So he muddies any clarity she's trying to establish.

*It was dark. I . . . I can't remember clearly.*

She shifts gear, puts a little pressure on the gas.

*It's not possible that you saw him. He was on the floor. You were on the bed. You would've had to lean right up and over to get a look at his head on the floor.*

So that's what she's going for, an inconsistency in his account? Really, that's her great detective mind at work? Surely she knows how hard it is to convict a murder case even with heaps of evidence. She has nothing and yet she's going for a little *gotcha* on his angle of vision from the side of the bed, even with his *maybe*s, *not sure*s, and *hard to remember*s?

Eric is a little disappointed. He knows this feeling. Ever since he was a child, he has built things up in his mind and imagined how exciting they would be. The anticipation is exquisite, and then the thing happens, and it never lives up to his expectations, and the bitter aftertaste hangs around. Like when he was six years old and dreamed of getting a fish to put in his bedroom. He imagined they would be friends, like *Nemo*. And then finally, after much harassing, his mother took him to get a goldfish, and he brought it home, and it just swam around in its dumb bowl and did nothing all day.

Or when he first went to Los Angeles in his twenties and he took the Hollywood bus tour that promised to show him where all the famous stars lived. He was so sure that he'd be able to make eye contact with some glamorous starlet and she'd see that they were kindred spirits and they should probably become fast friends. He spent over $200 on a new outfit just for the tour. But when he arrived, he found some overweight failed actor with a megaphone pointing at hedges and walls while he baked in the hot sun with a bunch of Chinese tourists on the open bus. Where was the glamour? Where was Hollywood? It was terrible. He hated every moment of it. He was in a funk for months after the trip to Los Angeles.

Then Mark came along with his good looks, his worship of Eric. He thought maybe he would finally be able to live the life that he had always desired, that he'd always felt he deserved. So he moved to be with Mark in Florida. Yes, Florida. It should have been a red flag, but Eric didn't see it, thought this was just a temporary pit stop before they eventually moved to New York.

But no, Mark actually liked Florida! Liked the people for their easygoing nature. And then he stopped working out and put on a few pounds. Eric felt the growing disdain, the metallic bitterness of an unremarkable and boring life returning. And he looked around at what was his life, at the fat, tasteless people of Jacksonville. And slowly that bitterness metamorphosed into a determination to change all of it. He would not accept this life. People only lived these kinds of pathetic lives because they accepted them. Not Eric; he refused to accept a banal existence like the one his mother lived, having to work so tirelessly to provide for them in some bullshit town in Bumfuck, Ohio, where the closest brush with glamour was the fact that Elvis had once driven through and taken a dump in one of the diner's bathrooms. *Fuck this,* thought Eric, and he'd stolen a bunch of his mom's jewelry and cash from her underwear drawer and taken a bus to Chicago.

Eric is used to disappointment and overcoming it. Like he did with the problem of Mark, and like he'll have to do with Detective Rose and her inability to provide the required gravity and expertise this moment requires.

*Like I said, it was dark, and I—it's hard to remember anything clearly . . . I don't want to remember . . . I'm trying to push those images out of my mind.*

Eric is slowly switching off. The scene is dragging, and he's bored now.

*If you don't mind, we need to send the lab to your apartment as well, to do a check on your phone and computer. Just routine stuff, so the upstairs people don't come down and ask, if you know what I mean.*

Does she understand who she's dealing with? thinks Eric. Have all those domestic violence brutes and sloppy drunks prevented her from seeing that Eric is no ordinary person, someone who would plan everything so meticulously but then leave incriminating evidence in such an obvious place as his computer and phone?

Detective Rose: just another disappointment in a long line of many disappointments in his life.

*Sure, I'm happy to help in any way I can.* He looks at her, hoping she can read a little of the *fuck you* in the delivery.

*Do you have any suspects? I heard there have been some gangs in the neighborhood recently.*

*Nothing yet, but we will get whoever did this. Don't worry, we always do.*

# thirty-eight

Someone is humming. He sounds happy. I've been in and out of consciousness for hours. I don't want to wake. I'm trying to take refuge in sleep, hoping that it will shelter me from the real world. But sleep is telling me that I've overstayed my welcome and that she won't keep me under her heavy blanket of unconsciousness for much longer. If I stay any longer, the dreams will only get more twisted, more uncomfortable, more suffocating. I look around the room; it's Cyril's. I've never been in here before, and now I'm sleeping in his bed. I remember the sleeping pills he offered. How long have I been here? The sun is high in the sky outside.

The humming . . .

I listen . . . It's not humming; it's singing in a low voice. It must be Jaya. How can he be singing? Singing isn't for the damned. Doesn't he know that I'm about to spend the rest of my life in jail?

I swing my legs over the bed. I see that I am wearing a pair of sweatpants and a T-shirt. I vaguely remember getting changed. Did Cyril speak with Jaya? I feel embarrassed, imagining what he might have said to him. *Something's very wrong with her. A broken person. I took her in.*

I cry in the shower until the water runs cold and my tears dry up.

I hear Cyril go off to work. It's just Jaya and me. I have to come out. I must try to function. Jaya is at the stove cooking something. He's leaning over the chopping board, dicing some parsley. Is that parsley? Something is boiling on the stove. It smells like real food, not things that come from packets or require defrosting and microwaving.

*Hare Krishna Hare Krishna*, he sings to himself.

*Hi.*

He turns around, sees me, and smiles. I feel my face collapsing in grief. I try to hold it in. He walks over and puts his arms around me. I thought that I had no more tears left, but I was wrong. He breaks the embrace after a few moments.

*I made some vegetable soup. Sit—I'll make you a bowl.*

He walks back to the stove, opens the cupboard above him, and takes out a bowl. He doesn't say anything about why I'm here or what Cyril must have told him. It's like he gets it and soup is the answer.

I eat the soup, and I realize that I'm starving. He watches me and smiles. Why is he smiling? Doesn't he know that pity is the appropriate feeling here? He gets up, brings the pot over, and ladles me some more soup without asking. He leaves the pot on the table and gets himself a bowl.

*To think there are some barbarians out there who actually don't like soup,* he says with a grin as he dips his spoon in his bowl.

We sit and eat in silence.

*Is Cyril at work?* I ask in a tiny voice.

*Yes, he says you should call him if you need anything. He'll be back at around six.*

The soup does something to me that I didn't think food could do. My emotional state is close to insanity, and I'm at the point of an irreversible breakdown, but still, I feel it reaches parts of me I haven't been able to access in years. It nourishes long-neglected chambers of my soul, and in some inarticulate way, I feel the faintest, most delicate string of hope. It has no reason to arise within me, and as soon as I try to grab onto it, it eludes me, like I'm trying to catch smoke. But still, it's something.

*Thank you for the soup.*

---

I sit on the balcony overlooking the traffic on the main road. The cars are noisy. But I'm grateful for the distraction, anything to stop the loop in my mind: the thud of the body on the bedroom floor, the blood, the glazed eyes. I try to watch the cars, look for order—people living their lives—but not for the man I killed. Panic, like a startled bird in a cage, desperately tries to escape the small space in my chest, fluttering and bashing its wings against my ribs. Will I go to jail? Will Em disown me? I try to calm down.

A flash of anger slices through me. What kind of person does that? Tricks a person into murder? I'm shocked at the clarity of my rage, but it's gone as quickly as it came. The fluttering, panicky bird of anxiety flies back in its place. Whereas my fear used to be encompassing, dull, and debilitating . . . now it's sharp and demanding.

*You'd better do something, or you will be going to jail for the rest of your life. You'd better find a way out of this.* It's like my mind has a new chew toy. Who? What? Why? And it won't let go until I provide satisfactory answers. I get to my feet. I can't sit still, restless-everything syndrome.

I want to drink, whiskey or vodka or something that means business, something to pacify the frantic trapped bird. I pull out my phone and start trawling news sites, looking for murder reports. I'm struck by how many there are, how much horror plays out each day. Spouse strangles wife. Dispute at bar, man stabbed. Gang drive-by shooting. Drunk driver plows into crowd. Drug deal gone wrong, three dead. College student raped and murdered in park. Elderly woman bludgeoned to death in apartment. And then I find it: *Atlantic Beach Police are investigating the shooting to death of a man early on Monday morning at his house on Oak Street.*

Like a truck has plowed into me, I see it in black and white, in the *Jacksonville Sun*: *Truth, truth, read all about it!* Mary murdered someone, and she's going to jail for the rest of her life and will never see her sweet, innocent daughter again. Truth, truth, read all about it!

I read on: *Officers responded to a 911 call on Oak Street at about 2 a.m. on Monday, the Atlantic Beach Police Department spokesperson said in a press release. They found Mark Matthews shot five times in his bedroom in what appears to be a break-in. Police received a call from Mark Matthews's partner, Eric Wilson. Officers performed CPR and continued lifesaving efforts until emergency services arrived, but the man died at the scene. The case remains under investigation.*

Eric Wilson? Not Eric Smith? I read it again: *Mark Matthews's partner, Eric Wilson.*

Oak Street. I was there.

*They found Mark Matthews shot five times.* I did that.

Each word is like a balled-up fist to the gut.

What have I done?

The frantic trapped bird is momentarily stunned by shock. It lies at the bottom of the cage, bloodied and bruised, feathers everywhere, wild eyes staring into the middle distance. The news report evaporates any lingering doubts in my mind about whether it really happened. It did. The man is dead, shot five times. I want to howl, but Jaya is here. I go into Cyril's room, roll into a ball on the bed, shove the sheet into my mouth. I scream, beat the pillows. The split in my soul tears, painfully, like a diamond cracking, something that shouldn't succumb but does because of an ungodly pressure. The crack lets in the searing light of pain that should never be in such a sensitive area. It's a cigarette put out in an eyeball. I scream, choke on the sheet. Maybe I can choke myself to death.

I hear noises.

Cyril is home.

I can't face Cyril. I try to breathe slowly to calm down. I'm red in the face and petrified. I hear mumbled voices in the other room. Are they talking about me? Of course they are. I hear footsteps coming toward the door.

Knock, knock.

*Go away, go away,* I scream in my head.

I close my eyes, pretending to be asleep. I hear the door slowly creep open. It's Cyril. I can feel him peering in. *Please, please just go away.* The door closes, and I hear the footsteps walk away and then more voices.

*She must be exhausted,* I think I hear him say.

And I am.

# thirty-nine

Detective Rose wants to talk to Eric again. Eric is going to comply. He knows there are only so many times they can call him in. If they keep doing this, calling him in and getting nothing, they are going to look incompetent, as if they are harassing him. But Eric will be patient. He's thought this through.

He sits in the reception area of the ugly police station. He's been here since 8:30 a.m. The place was quiet when he arrived. However, it's 10:00 a.m. now, and the station is a rolling boil of noise and people.

When he's finally led into the little room—the interrogation room they don't call the interrogation room, with its single desk and two mismatched chairs—Eric wonders if he's going to be able to keep his cool. He feels the first sign of fraying at the edges of his restraint.

Detective Rose makes him wait another twenty-five minutes before she enters the room.

*Sorry about the delay, Mr. Wilson,* she says as she sits down without looking at him.

Eric smiles his benign and tolerant Buddha smile. *Happy to help if I can.*

She starts flipping through some papers.
*Were you and Mark having any problems?*
*Problems?*
*Relationship problems.*
He was untidy, which really got to me, and our tastes differed, which did cause some problems, but you know, nothing we couldn't overlook.
*Your tastes differed?*
*Mark was more of a meat-and-potatoes man.*
She nods. *And you?*
*More white truffles and a late-harvest Carménère.* He smiles, sure that she has never had either and delighting in letting her know he is well aware of that. She smiles back.
*And that was the source of tension?*
They go back and forth. It's a dull game, and Eric starts to feel bored.
*Can you explain this?*
She's taken some papers from her folder and slid them across to him. He sees the look in her eyes, the imminent victory she wants to claim. But Eric is expecting more from her. Does she really think that he wasn't prepared for them to find Mark's insurance policy, naming Eric as the beneficiary? Surely she can't think that he's that stupid?
*This policy was only taken out two months ago.*
Eric looks up from the papers and manages with all the fake shock he can muster to ask, *Do you think he knew he was going to die?*
Oh boy! She's going to hate this, that he's pretending the policy is something they didn't discuss and that it's shockingly new to him.
*He named you as the beneficiary.*
Eric pushes out a tear. He wonders again if maybe acting is something he should seriously consider.

They go on like this for another two hours. Eric has to dig deep into his reserves of patience. He studies Detective Rose's face when she speaks, the broadness of the cheeks, the close-set eyes. He looks at her lilac short-sleeved blouse, the no-nonsense gold studs in her ears. He pictures her life: single of course, the drab apartment filled with TV dinners and nature shows. His dislike for her grows. He wants to taunt her, like some villain in a movie, but he doesn't. He answers whatever she asks. She finds nothing, and eventually he wins, like he knew he would.

*We may need to call you in again, so please notify the station if you plan on going anywhere.*

She gets to her feet. *Thank you for your time this morning, Mr. Wilson. We're doing all we can to find out who did this.*

He smiles appreciatively at the hardworking, poorly paid public servant that is Detective Rose.

———

*A what?* There's a vein protruding from Eric's forehead. He's standing in his home, with the phone to his ear, feeling his anger grow.

*A contestability period. There's a clause in the policy. It's standard, really. It reads: "In the event of a death within the first year,"* a reasonable voice tells him from the other end of the phone.

*So now what?*

*There will be an investigation into the cause of death and examination of the autopsy and toxicology reports and medical records.*

*The police are already doing that. He was shot in his home. On top of this you're telling me the insurance company is stalling. There's a fitting funeral to pay for. Have you no shame?*

*I'm sorry, Mr. Wilson, I truly am. We aim to expedite this in as timely a fashion as possible.*

*What's timely? How long before the payout?*

*Each case is a little different, but I imagine somewhere between three and six months.*

*No!* Eric stamps his foot on the floor like a child having a tantrum. He catches himself, slows down.

*There are expenses: his funeral; his mother has medical issues. We can't wait that long.*

*I understand.*

*This is an incredibly stressful time. Please don't delay any further.* Eric hangs up.

He wants to smash the phone on the wall, like Colin Farrell does in the thriller *Broken*. But he doesn't. Instead, he stands there, fuming inside. He's worried . . . This rage he has . . . Maybe he'll snap one day. Maybe he won't need a broken housewife to do his killing for him; maybe he will just do it himself.

Three months is too long. He knows that. Three more months dealing with that ugly policewoman, three more months in this cramped apartment, three more months in the Florida heat with the vest-wearing, Big Gulp–slurping, *y'all* yahoo locals, will drive him up the fucking wall. He has plans. New York first to meet with the designer of the bespoke tiki bar franchise that he's going to start in the Keys. High end, laid back; an HE/LB production. There will be a launch. Andy, his new business partner—and soon-to-be lover if all goes to plan—has a whole list of celebrities and influencers he can get to come.

He even mentioned getting Aurora to sing, but they would have to change the menu to go all vegan. Andy said it was a good idea. Everyone is going vegan these days. *It's trending all over, babes, think about it.* Eric did, for about two seconds. *We don't need Aurora.* Andy said he had someone who could get to Billie Eilish. Eric had to stop himself from wrinkling up his nose. Has Andy ever seen the clothes that she wears? Those neon-green, baggy football shirts? *Really, Andy, we're going to have to address some things if we're ever going to be lovers.*

Eric paces around his tiny kitchen, wondering when Mark's house will no longer be considered a crime scene so that he can move in. It's way more spacious. He's about to call the police and inquire about that when he hears a knock at the door.

# forty

It was surprisingly easy to find him and his address and phone number—his real address and his real phone number. Not the phone number we had previously communicated on, which he had now disabled. All I had to do was type his name into PeopleWhiz.com, and there it was. That was the easy part. The hard part was finding the courage to go and confront him.

Standing at his door now, I feel that courage slipping away, as if it's leaking through my shoes onto the tiles underfoot, dripping off the second-story landing and providing nourishment for the grass below.

My outrage drove me here. How dare he? But it drove me here on fumes, and now there is nothing left.

I'm about to leave when the door opens.

I see Eric's face transform into a strained smile.

*Hello, Mary. What a surprise to see you.*

I frown. Why is he smiling?

*How can I help you?*

*Why?* My voice is weak like jelly.

*Why what?*

*Why did you make me do that? Why me?*

There is only philosophy now. Why? Why everything? Why

does Emma have to suffer? Where does David's all-consuming rage come from? How is it sustained? Why, despite my efforts to live a good and kind life, do I have to suffer so much? Why did this man, Mark Matthews, have to die? Why did the Department of Children and Families come to my home at that inappropriate moment? Why do I get the sense that Jaya knows more suffering and more joy than I could ever know in a hundred lives? And yes, why did Eric trick me into doing such a terrible thing?

*I'm sorry, dear. I don't seem to understand. Why did I make you do what?*

I look at him. Something is wrong again. Who is this person?

*Why did you lie to me and make me kill him?*

I see his eyes widen theatrically.

*Kill who?*

I stare. I know what happened.

*You can't do this to me.*

*Are you okay, sweetie? I think you may be confused or something.*

*I'm going to tell the police.*

He smiles at me. I know that smile, patronizing, smug. The smirk of the unthreatened. I wonder if he's ever been on the receiving end of that smile. It's the kind of smile that very accomplished and intelligent women still get, the smile that says: *Look at you, going toe to toe with the big boys.*

*And tell them what, sweetie?* he asks.

He smirks again. His sarcasm is humiliating me. I made a terrible mistake coming here.

*Yes, you haven't really thought this through, have you.*

My shame coils around me like a serpent.

*The newspaper said he was your partner. Why did you want me to kill him?*

He looks at me. His eyes narrow. I don't mean that as an accusation. I genuinely want to know.

*I think you should leave now.*

Then his smirk changes. Patronizing smile number two, with an added dash of malice.

*If I ever see you again, I'll call the police myself.*

He gives me a little *toodle-oo* with his fingers and closes the door in my face. I stand there, the door an inch from my nose. The shame serpent is coiling around my throat now. I'm finding it hard to breathe. My mind is strangely blank. As if seized, too many gears and cogs turning at once.

He's lying, I have to remind myself. He's gaslighting me. *Hold on to truth, dear Mary. If that goes, there's nothing else left.*

I walk down the stairs in a daze, mildly amazed that some people seem to be able to get away with anything. A woman walks past me on the stairs. She's carrying a shopping bag in her hands. After she's passed me, I suddenly feel guilty for not asking if I could help her carry her bag. She looked around twenty, probably half my age, and it was only one bag. Why do I feel bad like that? Why do I feel so insecure, as if unless I'm helping other people, I am somehow at fault or not worthy of space in the world?

I sit at the bus stop and look down at my hands in my lap. *You're pathetic. What's wrong with you?*

David's angry words swim around in my head. David and his inarticulate fury that would fill the house for days and weeks. I don't know what is wrong with me, but Eric could see it clearly enough to manipulate me to do such a terrible thing. *What is wrong with Eric?* says the other voice, a little voice inside me that rarely speaks. It's a good question. It's a question Mary the Strong would ask.

A police car drives past. Will I go to jail? What will Emma think? An image of Jaya pops into my head, the big man with the child eyes and the vegetable soup. I remember the way he looked at me when I was crying, as if he had cried like that too once because life can be a tragedy, but he still believed we should make soup.

The bus arrives and hisses its doors open for me. I wait too long before climbing in, long enough for the bus driver to roll his eyes at another crazy he's going to have to deal with. I scurry up the stairs as if to make up for my delayed response. The door closes behind me, and we drive away. I have to grab the handrails as the bus jolts off.

The bus ride lulls me, my head vibrating against the window. I feel a distance from the horror that is my life now, like an onlooker taking in the charred remains of a wildfire that has swept through the life of Mary Williams. Everything is gone. She's lost it all. There's just the warm ash of her previous life squishing under her toes. Where there was once substance and the semblance of a woman with a job, an apartment, a daughter, and hopes and dreams, now there is nothing.

*my life*

*aflame*

*the*

*burning*

*pieces*

*fall*

*from the*

*sky*

*twisting*

*in the*

*hot     breeze*

*like*

*stoned*

*ballerinas*

*on*

*fire*

An image of the lily-like diamond flower drifts into my head, with its long thick waxed white leaves. I'm in Mrs. Knox's middle school geography class. She's droning on about the fauna and flora of California. *The diamond flower.* I like the name. I'm interested. Like a dog hearing a whistle somewhere, I perk up my ears. In the barren wasteland of Mrs. Knox's geography class, a little girl sees an oasis, something interesting.

*As extreme pressure creates a diamond, so extreme heat from wildfires is required to activate the diamond flower seeds.*

She shows us a picture, the waxy white flower stamen rising from the black ash of an inferno. It looks pure and spiritual. It looks like hope.

Something begins to stir in a place I have yet to name.

# forty-one

*You don't have to say anything you don't want to say, but if I can help with whatever is going on, I would like to. And of course, please, you can stay as long as you need.* Cyril smiles at me and squeezes my hand.
*Jaya will stay out of your way. He's not intrusive, don't worry.*

I want to defend Jaya immediately, tell Cyril I would never think that Jaya is an intrusion. I am the one who has barged into their life. But I don't say this. I don't know how to speak with Cyril. Too much has changed in too short a period of time. I don't know how to be around him. It was always him wanting me, desperate to please me, me rebuffing him, keeping a distance, making sure his expectations were kept in check. But now everything has changed. I need him, his home, his food, his hot shower. I have to talk to him about us . . . how I can't stay here with the expectation that we are a couple. I simply have no place to live. This is a desperate act of survival, not an escalation in the romance of our relationship. But I can't say that. I'm grateful, but giving him my body seems like it would wrong him as well as me. He's respectful and sensitive to my state, but we share the same bed, and he wants to cuddle. Pushing back that innocent gesture seems cruel, but I know he's a man: his hands will creep.

*I like Jaya. He's been kind to me.* But then I quickly add, *Like you have been.*

We share a look. Although he said he wouldn't, he asks, *What happened?*

*I—I just fell behind on the rent after I was let go from the library . . . and one thing on top of another . . . I'm going to David . . . I think I had some kind of a breakdown.*

He squeezes my hand again.

*I'm sorry I got you involved. I know this isn't your problem.*

*No, Mary, don't say that. I'm happy to help in any way I can.*

He is happy. I can tell that. Not at my misfortune but that I'm here with him; that one unattainable thing, the most alluring of all things, the thing you can't have, he now has right here. I wonder how much rage he has in him. I wonder if, when, it will come out. I make up a story about a friend being killed recently. A break-in. I need to explain my trips out, my Google searches, my compounded sadness. Thankfully, he doesn't pry too much. I notice Jaya looking at me from the stove. He's making olive bread. It smells good, fills the small apartment with life. Does he know I'm lying? Ever since Cyril told me Jaya was once a monk, I've felt the urge to confess everything to him.

*Emma—she, I mean, I—I have her every second Thursday, three to nine, until . . . you know, until the custody issues have been sorted out.*

*She can come here. We can do something together.* Cyril is spontaneously kind. I'm grateful.

*Thank you.*

*Oh, damn. I'm working this Thursday. That's okay; it'll probably be better the first time, anyway, if I'm not here so she can get used to the place.*

Cyril and Jaya are polite, not saying anything more, sensitive to the situation. I'm clearly a damaged woman and need to be treated delicately.

---

Cyril leaves for work, and I hide out in his room, afraid of having to make small talk with Jaya. Alone in the room, I pace. My mind is chewing hard on its new toy.

*Terror.*

It's just a matter of time before the police come knocking, before I'm taken away in handcuffs, my head lowered into the back of the waiting patrol car, nosy neighbors watching with feigned horror. I put Google Alerts on my phone. *Mark Matthews. Eric Wilson. Oak Street shooting.* I type *Mary Williams* and immediately wonder if this implicates me. I delete my name and put the phone down.

*Ping ping ping ping*

I scroll through all the alerts, but there's no new information. I put down the phone again. There's a new nausea in my stomach. The trapped anxiety bird drowning in an acidic terror broth.

I lie on the bed, and I try to slow breathe away the building fear.

# forty-two

Em comes over on Thursday. It's awkward. It was never awkward between us before. I dote on her while she does her homework. Cyril and Jaya are both out, so it's just us, but she doesn't want to talk about anything. I overcompensate, too eager to please. Finally, she looks at me.

*What are you doing?*

I have no answer. I laugh it off. Embarrassed again.

Can she sense my guilt? Does she intuitively know what I did?

I step out to get the washing from downstairs. I wait there a moment. I don't want to go back up, to Em, for her to see me like this, so rudderless, so unsure of how to be around her. It's distressing to her, I can tell, her mother not certain of how to be her mother anymore.

After some time, I force myself up the stairs. When I walk back inside, I see she's playing chess with Jaya. When did he get back? When did he start playing chess?

*Oh, hi, you're back,* I say as casually as I can.

*You might not want to watch this part, though—the part where young Emma gets squashed,* Jaya says.

*Yeah, right.* She moves her knight to F6. *Check.*

Jaya sits up. *You don't know what you're dealing with, Mr. Jaya,* I think to myself.

*You're a bit young to be carrying around that kind of attitude, young lady.*

*You might not want to watch this part, Mom. He's about to go down.*

Jaya smiles. *You didn't tell me she could play.*

*I didn't know you play.*

*Of course, it's the perfect game. It's the only game that has no element of luck. That's unless you count Emma's unluckiness in challenging somebody who so clearly has superior skill.*

Em loves this, the good-natured trash talk. It's typically too pandering and patronizing from encouraging adults. Or it's too aggressive and mean spirited from her teenage peers. Jaya hits the perfect note with her. I want to cry: hope, a green seedling on the barren tree of my good fortune.

*I'm going to put the bread in the oven. Watch that she doesn't cheat,* Jaya says as he gets up.

Em glances at me, and I give her a thumbs-up. It's too eager and ruins the mood. *Just be chill,* her eyes tell me. I go and lie down on the bed. Cyril's bed? Our bed?

*Breathe.* I stare at the ceiling. *Just be chill, Mary, just be chill awhile.*

———

I'm in the middle of a fire. The crackle and pop of the inferno is near deafening, but somehow, I'm not burning. The flames are crawling up my legs, but my limbs are white, waxy like the diamond flower, impervious to the blaze. I feel stronger than I've felt for a lifetime, as if flames *can't* burn me. I'm too strong for them. I am Mary the Strong. It's near elation. I hear the low drone of someone singing, hymns of praise . . . Praise of me? Of my strength?

And then my eyes blink open. I must've fallen asleep. The dream lingers, the residue of strength remaining in my heart. I want to go to Emma, show her I'm strong. Show her I'm not her needy friend. I'm her mother. I'm here for her. I walk out to the living room. Jaya has his back to me. He's sitting there playing the harmonium on the floor and quietly singing in his low voice:

*Hare Krishna Hare Krishna . . .*

He senses me and turns.

*Hey, Emma left. She didn't want to wake you.*

I look at him. He looks at me. I'm grateful to him for saving the day without even knowing it. I want to tell him about my dream, about the diamond flower and my strength, but I don't.

*She won. She's feisty.* He smiles.

*Yeah, she's a good player.*

*There's some fresh olive bread and hummus if you like.*

I have to tell him. I have to tell Jaya about Eric Wilson. I have to tell Jaya what I did.

But I can't. How do you tell someone you did something like that?

He's on the balcony now, putting soil in the pots of some new plants he bought. I watch him as I chew on his olive bread. His olive and sun-dried tomato and basil and salt and some other things, unimaginably tasty bread. Could I ever do this, bake bread? Is this what healthy normal people do? Jaya transplants a small bundle of tiny yellow flowers into a larger pot. The roots are tangled in clumps like witches' knotted hair. He runs his fingers through the roots gently, separating but not breaking them. Dark black soil falls onto his pale thigh.

My phone pings. It's a Google Alert.

# forty-three

Finding appropriate clothes wasn't as hard as I expected. Neither was finding the nerve to go. How so? How did I just decide I would go? Am I strong? Have I always been strong?

Mary the Strong, slowly emerging from the horror. It's the right thing to do, to pay respects. Mary the Strong wants to do the right thing. Cyril lends me a black jacket. It's a little too thick for the sunny weather, but it's all he has. There's a bus that takes me and drops me only a block away. As I get off and walk toward the gathering, I know that this is the right thing to do. If you make a mistake, the first thing you should do is say sorry, my mother used to say.

———

Eric likes that he's the center of attention. Technically, Mark is, but Mark's dead, so all eyes are on him, the grieving lover. He likes the way he looks in black too. It gives him a certain gravitas, a certain substance. All that's needed is some gray clouds and rain bouncing off the coffin for this to be some scene out of a French movie. But it's not raining. It's Florida sunny, and he feels awkward seeing all of Mark's friends, who he barely knows. Mark's mother is here too, in her wheelchair with her depressed face, and she's wearing gray, not black. He looks around at the sorry bunch. And then he sees her, standing under the tree fifty feet away, wearing a too-big black jacket.

*Bitch,* he says, under his breath. *What the fuck is she doing here?*

---

People are walking past the open grave and throwing in flowers. I join the line. I can see Eric is glaring at me, but I have to do this. A young woman is pushing an old lady in a wheelchair in front of me. I want to offer help, but I don't. The old woman has a coughing fit, and the young woman comes around to the front of the chair to see if she's okay. My turn comes, and I take the flowers I picked on the walk from the bus stop, stretch my hand over the recently dug grave, the dark sides of the earth looking wet and alive, and slowly let the little flowers scatter through my fingers. I watch them tumble through the air and bounce softly off the coffin. I close my eyes and whisper in my head:

*I'm sorry. I thought I was trying to help someone. I'm so very sorry. Please forgive me.*

I feel something. Like understanding. I want to linger. I want to pray harder, deeper, confirm this feeling that I might be getting, but I'm aware of the child behind me, fidgety and restless. I move off.

I realize the old woman in the wheelchair is Mark Matthews's mother. She has a look on her face that throws me. She's stricken with grief, crushed by it. No mother should ever bury her son. It's unnatural, and all that unadulterated pain covers her face like an acid blush. Instead of enhancing, it is taking away her beauty, her life; she doesn't glow but darkens.

I did this to her. Yes, it was a mistake, but I pulled the trigger. Six times. Did I really shoot that gun six times? I have almost no memory of walking into the room. And now he's dead, and she sits there, bent over in her wheelchair, heartbroken and shattered.

I want to speak to her. It's near impossible for me to see that kind of suffering and not want to help. And when I'm the cause of her suffering, the urge is almost unstoppable. I start to walk over to her, but suddenly Eric is right in front of me. He is smiling, but there's something wrong with the smile. It doesn't match his eyes. His eyes are cold and fierce. He takes my arm and pulls me off to the side. It hurts. He still has that smile on his face as he talks with clenched teeth, with his back to the grave and the mourners.

*What are you doing here? This event is not open to the publ—*

He stops midsentence. There's a commotion around the graveside. Someone is shouting, *Call 911.*

I'm bewildered. Eric sees what's going on, and he rolls his eyes derisively. I look over at the grave site. The old woman, Mark's mother, has fallen out of her wheelchair. People are backing up to give her some air. Someone is crying. Eric is walking over, annoyed. I don't know whether to go or leave.

―――

The sirens of the ambulance are too loud, and the ambulance is driving too fast over the grass in the cemetery. It seems out of place and undignified. I stand around with a group of women, watching as the medics perform CPR on Mark Matthews's mother. They seem to be pushing too hard on her chest. Will they break her bones?

Joyce Matthews has chronic diabetes and has been in and

out of the hospital for the last several years. She loved Mark very much. Mark was her only son, and he had been taking care of her since her husband died over ten years ago. She didn't know that Mark was gay, and she continuously tried to set him up with single women. Her medical conditions were slowly killing her, though, and even with Mark helping her, she was anxious that the diabetes would either bankrupt her or cause her premature death. I heard all of this from the women I was standing with while the medics were treating Joyce, trying to get her onto the gurney and into the ambulance. She used to knit scarves for the homeless, but since her health had taken a turn for the worse, she hadn't been able to knit as many as she had previously.

*She is a sweet person,* says an older woman with dark glasses and sagging skin around her neck.

*So positive,* says another. *Mark dying like that . . . it did something to her, though.*

*Tragic,* says Dark Glasses.

Then a shorter, stockier woman pipes up, *I hope they catch whoever did this. They should hang him from the nearest goddamn tree, I tell you. What kind of animal does something like this?*

I want to drop to my knees and confess. How could I not? The anxiety bird has escaped its cage and is now flying blindly inside my chest. Manic wings beat against my rib cage. I feel my hands starting to tremble.

*She's got nothing now—no one,* says the short one as she turns and walks off, punctuating the finality of her statement.

*Where are they taking her?* I blurt out.

*Probably St. Mary's,* someone replies without looking at me.

# forty-four

Detective Rose has an oil painting in her office painted by her son. It's cubist. A woman with fingers for hair and flowers for her ear. It's about the only thing in her office that has no workplace functionality.

She has it up it there because he gave it to her. But the painting makes no sense to her. Why deliberately add confusion; why make abstract what was once clear? she often wonders while looking at it. Her job is the opposite: take random things and put them in order, put them together so they fit. She doesn't take things that are together and break them apart. She does like art, though, and she often imagines herself retired and painting watercolors of the sun setting at the beach in Daytona. She wonders what that would be like, just letting things be, the unsolved things, things that are out of place. Could she turn away from that—just paint a watercolor of the sea instead? It's uncomfortable for her to imagine not trying to put things in order. *Is art indulgent?* she wonders. Is art that thing that comes *after* order, a leisurely pursuit, earned *after* one's duties have been done? Maybe the thing she—

*He's here.* A head pops into her office, interrupting her train of thought.

She grabs a folder from her desk and follows the officer down the corridor into the same interrogation room where she questioned Eric Wilson. There's a man in a chair, late fifties, heavyset, looks tired.

*Hello, Mr. Brown. Thank you so much for coming to speak with us.*

*Is it my son? What'd he do?*

*No, nothing like that, Mr. Brown. There was a murder on Oak Street at around two a.m. on Monday the fifth, and we've been trawling through cameras from the traffic lights and the CCTV footage from some of the stores in the nearby area, trying to get a sense of who was around the neighborhood at that time.*

She slides the photos across to Mr. Brown.

*We picked up your license plate dropping off this woman—* she taps on a blurry image of someone getting out of a car—*at around two a.m. on the morning in question. This was just outside Mia Bo. According to Uber records, her name is Mary Williams and she was your last ride that night. Do you remember her at all?*

Mr. Brown thinks, squints at the photo, takes his time, then: *White? Nervy type?*

*I don't know. You tell us. Did she come across as nervous to you?*

*Her eyes, you know, looking around, like a little bird. Restless like—fidgeting a lot.*

*Anything else?*

Mr. Brown drums fingers on the table, thinking.

*Was there a person waiting for her? Did you get a chance to see which way she headed after you dropped her off?*

He shakes his head and looks up. *I don't remember anything like that. I barely remember her. Just edgy, you know? Nervous.*

Detective Rose nods, knows they're done here. She hands him a card.

*Please, if you remember anything—the smallest detail—it could be a great help to us. Please call.*

*She a murderer?* Mr. Brown's interest is piqued.

*No, we don't think she did anything. She might've seen something, though. We're really just looking at anything that might help,* Detective Rose explains.

Mr. Brown gets up to leave. Detective Rose sits with the black-and-white screenshots of the surrounding streets and shops and houses of Oak Street, hoping to find something, trying to put the pieces together, the anticubist.

Officer Lewis sticks his head into the office a few minutes later. *I might have something.*

Rose looks up. She knows that tone. It's a good tone.

———

Officer Lewis and Detective Rose step out of the car. They're with David Aguilera, late thirties, preppy, neat looking, wearing some kind of scout shirt with many pockets. He has a cell phone holder on his belt. He's talking at a steady clip:

*As soon as I read about it, I did some cross-referencing with the neighborhood watch reports of that morning. I'm not block captain for this area. I cover Eleventh to Twentieth Street, but I'm the northwest coordinator, so I have access to that data. I found something that seemed like actionable intelligence, thought I should get you guys involved. I'm probably going to be the group's law enforcement liaison officer next year as well, so you know . . . good to get familiar with the systems of how you guys are working, you know, your MO and such.*

They walk toward an apartment block next to the alleyway. There's a dumpster at the end of the alley.

*So this is where he saw him.* David points to the edge of the alley. *We're talking approximately half a klick from Oak Street. Why don't you guys take a look around, and I'll go and get the witness.*

Detective Rose nods, and she and Lewis move over to the dumpster while David trots off toward the apartment block entrance.

Rose looks around the area, the main road lined with shops to the north, suburban houses to the west and south.

David's witness is an old gentleman in black slacks and a white short-sleeved shirt with a gold logo on his chest pocket. He puts out his hand.

*Lawrence Goldman. Pleased to meet you.*

*Detective Rose, and this is Officer Lewis. Can you tell us what you saw?*

David takes a step back, putting his hands behind his back and looking at the ground to make a show of giving the man's eyewitness account its due deference, as Lawrence Goldman begins to explain.

*More like what I heard: the sound of trash cans being knocked over. I got up to see cans scattered around the alley and someone getting to their feet and bolting out of there like someone was chasing them or they saw a ghost or something.*

*Did you get a look at his face?*

*I think it was a woman.*

David looks up. Did he miss this part? Detective Rose perks up too.

*I only saw her from the back. I was up there, second-floor balcony, looking down as she was running away. It looked like she was wearing a dress.*

*You sure?* inquires Officer Lewis.

*Can't be sure. It was dark, and she was running away from me. All I really got was the dress, but maybe it wasn't a dress. Maybe it was just a coat or something. I don't know.*

*What time was this?*

David takes a step back into the group of men.

*He called it in at nine past two in the a.m.*

*Nine past two?* Lewis crinkles up his nose at the turn of phrase.

*Two oh nine.*

Lewis nods. *Just say that.* He tells Detective Rose: *Preliminary reports are showing a time of death of two a.m. If a person was running from the crime scene for half a mile, they would arrive here just after two.*

*Do you remember the hair? Was it long, short?*

Goldman shakes his head. *Maybe short? It was pretty dark down there.*

A woman with short hair in a dress? Rose doesn't like this. It reminds her of her son's paintings. The parts that don't fit. The person who killed Mark Matthews is Eric Wilson. She was sure of that the moment she first spoke with him. For some bizarre reason, he was almost goading her to try to catch him. Rose knows she's seen the final picture of the puzzle, but she'll only get a judge and jury to see that same picture if she provides them with the right pieces. And this piece—a woman? It doesn't fit.

# forty-five

The receptionist at the front desk of the hospital is squeezing as much information about Joyce Matthews as she can out of me. They're concerned about who's going to pay for this. The young woman is torn between trying to show appropriate empathy and making sure that the hospital services are paid for. She's too young to have the nuance required to sufficiently navigate these opposing forces. On one side, ruthless capitalism and on the other, kindness. I feel for her. I want to say, *It's okay. You are just doing your job.* I want to tell her, *It's going to be okay.* But I don't because I'm not sure it will be anymore. Maybe in a few years' time, she could end up like me: homeless. Maybe she needs to start finding a way to boost her fortitude to deal with the potential devastation that may very well befall her. She has a poster of two kittens playing with a ball of yarn behind her. *Life's a ball,* it says. I'm thinking of telling her to take the poster down because it's very misleading. Particularly here in a hospital, a place where life is very much not "*a ball.*"

Joyce Matthews is awake when I go in to see her. I tell her that I was a friend of Mark's. I tell her how fondly he used to speak about her. Tears roll down her face, but there's a smile there too.

*Such a sweet, sweet boy.*

She takes my hand. Her skin is soft and loose, and the blue veins protrude noticeably from her wrist. She squeezes my fingers gently and says nothing. I notice a large red rash over the side of her body and right arm. It looks painful, the skin raised in welts. She tells me to come closer.

*When will I have to leave the house?* she asks.

I don't understand what she means.

*Who will pay the mortgage now that Mark is gone?*

Her expression distorts with worry.

*What about my treatments, and who will pay for the medicine?*

I'm looking down at my own face, the fear, the anxiety bird let loose inside, the terror of what the future holds.

Somehow, I find a smile. *Everything will be okay, Mrs. Matthews,* I lie.

I don't know where it comes from, but I know it's what I have to say. I know it's the only thing to say. She squeezes my hand again, harder, more desperately this time.

She looks at me with watery cataract eyes and asks, *Why— why did God take him like that?*

———

The doctor introduces himself and starts talking to me about Joyce. He seems distracted and doesn't look at me, instead reading the clipboard at the foot of the bed as he talks. He says that Joyce is running a substantial risk of kidney failure brought on by chronic type-two diabetes.

*She should be on hemodialysis.*

He wants to know why she isn't. He seems irritated with me.

I try to explain my relationship with her, that I'm not family. I try not to break down. I try to understand what he is saying. He looks up at me, clearly making some quick calculations in his head about the value of further time spent explaining things to me. He decides it's not worth it, says something about me speaking with the treatment coordinator, and then leaves. His white coat flaps against his legs as he strides out the door.

I look down at Joyce. The folds of her closed eyelids twitch. A machine pings softly somewhere in the room. She looks very pale, like there's not much left in her and what's left is escaping from a slow puncture.

I hold her hand.

*I'm sorry,* I whisper. *I'm so sorry.*

# forty-six

Jaya has a small makeshift altar in his bedroom. It's really a piece of wood placed on two bricks on the floor and then covered with a cloth. The altar is decorated with little yellow flowers that he grows on the balcony and a picture of an old Gandhi-like man smiling back at us. There's a small pile of gray ash from a burnt incense stick and a small tea light that seems to have been lit a while ago, the small flame dancing in a pool of hot wax.

Jaya is not here, though. I look out toward the balcony. The little yellow flowers in the potted plants drink in the afternoon sun. His room is neat and sparse with a single bed, neatly made, and a small table with a few books on top. I want to linger in there. I feel like a detective, not one trying to figure out the details of a crime but one trying to figure out if there are any really happy people in the world. Jaya seems the most likely suspect.

I look down at the books on his table:

*My Balcony, My Oasis: Gardening Tips for Balconies and Window Boxes.*

I pick up another book:

*Hold Your Own*, by Kae Tempest.

I flip through it. It's a collection of poems.

*When time pulls lives apart,
Hold your own.
When everything is fluid and when nothing can
be known with any certainty,
Hold your own.*

*Hold your own?* Can I do that, in the face of this impossible situation? I see the last book. It has a cover showing a woodcut print of an archer with a bow and a bag of arrows at his feet. His distraught head is in his hands. It's an old copy of the Bhagavad Gita. I have this book! Not this old version but the new one. I feel an instant connection with Jaya. I remember asking him how he was doing one day, and he said that he was *fighting the good fight.*

I'm startled as someone knocks at the front door. My nerves are raw. I want to ignore it. I can't face people—people whose normalcy will just highlight the horror that has become my life. They knock again. I hesitate and then get to my feet, straightening Jaya's bedsheet before I leave his room.

There's an old woman at the door.

*I think your fella needs some help.*

I don't know what she means. She has a grin on her face that confuses me too. I want to ask some clarifying questions, but I don't know where to start.

*He's out back near the recycling bins.* She gives a little snort and walks away. I stand there at the open door in a confused funk as if I've just woken up.

―

I find Jaya lying on the ground on his back, half inside the recycling area and half out. His jeans are dirty at the knees, and his phone is lying on the damp grass. His shirt is wet and stained. His eyes are closed but he's moaning. There's a potent, foul smell of booze and urine.

I see it's clearly Jaya, but a part of me doesn't recognize him, the sweet man who lives with Cyril and plays chess with my daughter, the stranger I feel compelled to confess my sins to. Seeing him in this state, I'm afraid because I know instinctively what this is. This is a man suffering. That pain can afflict even people like Jaya so acutely makes me afraid. He groans again.

I drop to my knees next to him.

*Jaya*, I say to him.

He moans something. I shake his arm a little. He opens his eyes. He takes a moment to see who I am, and then he starts crying.

*Mary, Mary, Mary . . . sho sorry what happened to you, oh, Mary, shish place . . . so shorry.*

He's slurring. It's hard to understand what he's saying. It takes a long time to get him upstairs to the apartment. He stumbles several times, and I knock my elbow hard on the steps. A UPS guy kindly offers to help me get him inside. He makes a joke about how not every day is going to make the highlight reel.

I've never seen a man cry like that, such a big burly man crying, convulsing in the fetal position on the living room floor. I try to tell him that everything will be okay, but I'm pretty sure that even in his obliterated state, he doesn't believe it. His intoxication fuels a remorse in him that I had no idea he had. It should comfort me that everyone is going through a hard time, but it doesn't. I feel vulnerable. If he can go down like this, what hope lies ahead for me?

He's asking for something, pointing to his room.

*Door, door,* he keeps saying, but I don't understand. I get him some water, and he knocks it over trying to drink it.

*Door.*

He's frustrated, spluttering.

DRAWER!

I go over to the bedside table and open the drawer he has been pointing at. There are earplugs, some British coins, chanting beads, and a bottle of pills. Jaya makes some noise of affirmation. That must be what he wants. I bring the pills over. He's clumsy as he gets three into his palm. He spills nearly half the bottle on the floor. I pick up the pills and try to close the lid.

*Pleash, soup, frishh.*

*Please. Soup. Fridge.* I understand drunk now. I get to my feet, take the soup from the fridge, and put it on the stove. He's trying to sober up.

———

Sometime later, Jaya has eaten, showered, and gone to bed. Cyril has come and gone. There's a rehearsal tonight. I told him that Jaya wasn't feeling that well. He said he was glad that I was there to help. He asked me if I wanted to go watch his group rehearse for their upcoming play. It's Shakespearean, he said. I said I should probably stay around in case Jaya took a turn for the worse. I felt bad. I could see his disappointment. I almost changed my mind, just went with him, to make him happy for all he was doing for me, but I didn't. Jaya woke up about twenty minutes after Cyril had gone. He called out for me. He was contrite. He looked like a schoolboy who had been caught stealing sweets from the shop. He sat up in bed.

*Thank you . . . for helping me.*

*Yes, of course. No problem.*

I'm trying desperately not to say trite bullshit things. I want to tell him I understand completely. I want to tell him what I did and how my own guilt is killing me. I want to tell him that he shouldn't feel ashamed, that we're in this together: him, me, everyone. We're all just trying to make this work.

Instead, I say, *Think nothing of it.*

He looks at me, some clarity slowly returning to his eyes.

*I made a mistake. Some time ago, I made a mistake that I have been struggling to forgive myself for ever since.*

I want to wrap my arms around him. I want to mother this little boy in a sixty-year-old body. He wants to tell me what happened. He wants to explain his pain. I nod. He looks at me, reading me, and then he starts.

One time when he was about six, he and his family went to the beach for a day. They played in the waves. He and his dad built a huge sandcastle with a moat and found a conch shell with a smooth pink inside and a pointed nose. They spent the whole day there, playing in the sea, eating apple pie and cream under the tent on the beach. It was one of the best days he could remember. On the way back home, they drove past a young Black boy, around his age, scratching in the bins for food. He was dressed in a thick, ragged coat. Seeing this, Jaya's whole mood changed, and he felt a terrible sadness that stayed with him during the whole ride back. Somehow, since then, he had the idea that he couldn't be happy while other people were suffering. When he was eighteen, not needing permission from his parents anymore, he moved into a Krishna temple in Oregon to be a monk. He wanted to learn how to help people.

After fifteen years, he took vows of celibacy and detachment and became one of the youngest and most distinguished teachers of the Krishna movement. He traveled around the world lecturing and teaching younger monks. He had found his calling. He studied the Vedic teachings deeply, trying to understand the nature of suffering and how to solve this perennial problem of the world. He did whatever he could to help others, even at great personal expense and discomfort, often going the extra mile to try to make a difference in someone's life. He founded *Food for Life*, the feeding arm of the movement, which distributed sometimes as many as ten thousand meals a day in the slums of Delhi. Jaya himself rose at four in the morning to cook huge pots of rice and beans and only went to bed just before midnight, after having cleaned and arranged everything again for the next day's service.

And then one day a young Australian girl came to see him at the ashram. While backpacking around the Himalayas, a friend had given her a TED Talk to listen to. It was Jaya speaking about empathy. She had had an epiphany that she should find him and become his student. She was a wide-eyed, simple girl eager to learn. Jaya took her in and began to try to train her formally. Slowly, though, she became attracted to him, and they started a relationship. Racked with guilt at having broken his vows, Jaya went to his spiritual authorities and confessed. They told him to break it off with her and go to the center in Nairobi to distance himself and perform the necessary penance. The young girl didn't take it very well. She pleaded with him. She said God had spoken to her and had sent Jaya to help her. She had given up her life to serve his cause, and while helping him, she had given her body too, and he simply couldn't abandon her. Jaya was torn. He had dedicated his life to helping people and had seen her grow from a bewildered and depressed young girl into a competent and valuable member of the Food for Life team, expanding the program into dozens of new villages in North India. But he knew that although it would be painful for him and for her, he had to go. And so one night, he left.

The young girl turned on him. She accused him of sexually

abusing her and the leaders of trying to cover it up. She went to the press in India and got hold of reporters in Australia. She spread the story as far and wide as she could. The leaders went after the girl, sharing her record of previous mental health issues. Jaya was devastated. His spiritual leaders encouraged him to take some time away from lecturing in public and to go deeper into a life of study and prayer.

And then Jaya received the news that the girl had committed suicide. She left a note:

*I love you, Jaya.*

Her parents blamed the leaders for their callous treatment of their daughter. They blamed Jaya too. He resigned from his position and made a public statement accepting all the responsibility. The leaders stood by him, and they begged him not to leave, but he felt he had no choice.

He went to Thailand and lived on the beach permanently drunk for nearly two years until one day a young boy came up to him and told him that it was time for him to be kind to himself again. Jaya didn't know who the boy was or if he had been hallucinating, but somehow, he realized that the little boy was right and that he had to stop his self-destruction. He had to be kind to himself.

He went back to the US, stopped drinking, and started working for a nonprofit. He says he looked back on the experience with deep gratitude. He was naive and egocentric. He thought that he could help people. He didn't realize that he had no such ability. Everything had been arranged by providence, not him, and being free from the burden that he was somehow responsible for the well-being of everyone around him is the most liberating feeling he has ever known. He knows that he can still try to help where he can and that it is his nature to do so, but ultimately, he realizes that there are bigger things at play that are not under his control. He is absolved of solving the problem of the world.

He tells me that he is happy.

His relationship with the divine is sweeter than it has ever been, even when he was meditating eighteen hours a day as a young monk. He says he believes with all his heart in a kind, sweet, and loving God. It's just that sometimes—like a mother sometimes has to give her child bitter medicine when he's sick to cure him—providence has to hurt us to help us. He says that some days, however, he thinks about that young girl and her death, and his heart breaks all over again, and it's unbearable. The last time he got drunk like this was six years ago. He tells me he's sorry I had to see him like that. He isn't embarrassed. He says that it isn't good to pose as something you're not.

He stops speaking, and I can see that he feels better. I want to hug him, but then I realize I don't need to. He is getting nourishment from a deeper place than I can access.

We don't speak for some time, until I eventually turn to him and ask if I can tell him something. He smiles and says sure.

And then I tell him what I did.

I tell him everything.

# forty-seven

*I've been rather cooperative with you, Detective Rose. Is this not the fourth time that I've come down to the station or you've come to question me here? You've had the police scour every corner of my apartment, my computer, and my phone. What else do you want? I'm beginning to feel this is harassment.*

They're inside Eric's small apartment. He contemplated not letting them in. Detective Rose is there with her pinch-faced sidekick, Officer Lewis. He doesn't have to let them in. He knows that if they actually had any evidence—which they don't—they would have charged him long ago. She would have loved that, thinks Eric. That's probably how she gets off, handcuffing a handsome man who would otherwise never even look in her direction.

But it's a slow day, and he decided to let them in. Maybe he can goad Pinch Face into getting flustered again by answering his questions with cryptic questions of his own. *LOL.*

Detective Rose and Officer Lewis sit side by side on the sofa. Eric sits to the left in a high-backed chair that he spotted in an antique store on Main Street and bought with Mark's credit card.

*It's an ongoing murder case, Mr. Wilson. It's our duty to Mr.*

*Matthews and his loved ones that we pursue the leads to wherever they take us.*

*Well, do you have anything, anything at all? Did you investigate the gang that was in the neighborhood? What about Mark's ex-boyfriend who I told you about, Steven? That creepy guy from Queens who kept phoning?*

He looks at them, waiting for an answer. Detective Rose looks over at Officer Lewis. Officer Lewis finally takes a photo from an envelope and hands it to Eric.

*Do you know who this woman is?*

Eric looks down at the picture of Mary. It's from the funeral. He wants to vomit.

He sees Lewis look at his boss.

*Um, yes.*

Eric wasn't sure whether they would ever get this far, and he didn't give the same preparation to this scenario that he did to others; but still, he knows the game plan. He just needs to calm the fuck down and act normal. He didn't kill Mark Matthews, and there's nothing Pinch Face and his partner can do that's going to change that.

*Who is she?* inquires Detective Rose.

He wonders if now is the time to call the lawyer, the one who he previously consulted with, the expensive, handsome one. It would certainly add some desperately needed glamour to this drab affair with McKay & McKay's glass-walled conference rooms and their tailored suits.

*That's Mary Williams. She's an acquaintance.*

He decides against the lawyer and his expensive retainer. Secretly, though, he's impressed at how much lawyers value their time. He wonders what he would charge if he were a lawyer.

*An acquaintance?*

*(Don't just repeat what I'm saying, you broad-faced bitch. Ask*

*your fucking question.) Yes, she was helping me with some care I needed.*

He leans back a bit into his chair, takes a sardonic pause, and looks out the window as if he has other things on his mind—a man of multitudes.

People can say what they want about him, but he knows how to deal with the world, how to give as good as he got. He doesn't take shit from others, especially the two in front of him, who are about as much fun as a dose of herpes. But what about Mary Williams? He told her what to say if there was ever some connection made between him and her, but can she play her part? Was his gaslighting a step too far? Even with the threat of going to jail for the rest of her life hanging over her head, will she be able to keep her mouth shut and just follow the script he told her to follow?

However, even in the worst-case scenario, it's a complication and nothing more. Mary Williams killed Mark Matthews. Not him. And that is the fact. As he planned.

They have nothing.

*What care was that?*

*I have a personal health issue*, he says, daring her to pry further.

Officer Lewis's phone rings. He excuses himself and walks toward the door to take the call.

*Your phone records indicate that you made contact with her on the Friday two days before the murder.*

There is no question here, and Eric is sure as hell not going to make it easier for her, so he just sits there, subtly antagonizing her.

*What was that in connection with?*

*As I mentioned, it was a personal health issue.* Eric wants to smile; well, actually, he wants to smirk. He wants her to know what he thinks of her and her gray Crocs. *(Gray Crocs! Really? Are you trying to look as depressing as you possibly can?)*

Detective Rose gets to her feet when Lewis returns to the room.

*Thank you again for your time, Mr. Wilson. We appreciate it. We will let you know of any developments.*

---

Detective Rose asks Lewis to drive. She wants to think. Although, technically, she knows this is not really thinking; it's allowing the thoughts in her mind to wash over her, like the sea lapping onto the beach and then slowly receding back into the ocean. Sometimes the tide leaves behind a shell, a small dead fish, a bottle cap, something that comes from another place. She once tried to explain the process to Officer Lewis when she could see how uncomfortable her silences made him. She told him that she didn't like to think; she preferred to observe her mind thinking, to let it do the work, and then she came along later, walking down the beach at low tide, seeing what was washed up. Lewis didn't understand, and her attempt to explain the process seemed to make him more uneasy, not less. But he found a rare thread of humor and said he thought she spent too much time alone and should get a dog.

But Detective Rose knows it works. It's an art, though, to know when to resist sticking in your hand when you see something, to resist rushing clumsily into the shallows because you think you noticed something glinting under the surface of the water. You have to be patient. You have to let the universe do its thing. Some things get sucked back into the ocean, and some things are left on the beach. There's a difference. Some things have value, and some things are just sea trash. She knows that articulating this just makes her seem like a weirdo, but it works for her. Still, Lewis is right about her spending all her time alone, but she would never get a dog. They're too simple. She's warming to the idea of a cat, though.

*That was Aguilera. He thinks he might have something more. He's double-checking, and then he would like to meet us again.*

She nods okay.

She thinks of that smirk. The audacity of evil men, like Nicky Valdez, abuser, rapist, murderer. And now Eric Wilson— the same smirk. How can they live so untouched by their actions? Where in all God's green earth is the justice? Should she take up her gun, put aside the law, be a good person, and do something to stop evil?

She has no answer for this question. The sand is bare of washed-up revelations.

For now.

# forty-eight

Jaya listens as I tell him everything. He occasionally asks a question.
*Do you still have the text messages?*
I do, but there is nothing specific. I've checked. In hindsight, it's clear Eric planned this all to avoid incriminating himself in the slightest.
*Did anyone see you?*
I don't think so.
But mostly, he just listens. Somehow, I manage not to break down. I speak for nearly an hour, and when I'm finished, he doesn't say anything. We just sit in his room. He's still in bed but seems to be feeling better.
After a long moment he says, *Wow . . . you win,* and then he laughs.
Surprisingly, I do too. I'm not even sure why we laugh, but we do, and for the briefest of moments, things are okay.
*I'm here to help you. We'll figure this out.*

Cyril comes back from his theater practice. I make a pasta salad, and we eat together. Jaya is still in his room. Cyril is happy and excited to tell me how the rehearsals are going.

*Harold is brilliant, just so intense.*

I know who he's talking about, the thin guy with the mustache, their resident Daniel Day-Lewis.

*I wish I could—you know—go for it like that. I try. I just don't have it, like, that . . . Aaargh!* He shakes his fork and laughs.

I'm glad to see him happy. I'm glad I cooked for him. He's been kind to me. I thank him again for letting me stay here. I smile, and I hope he can't see the terror running through me.

Later in bed, I feel his hands creeping. I knew this was coming, and I know there's no way out of this without hurting his feelings. I'm too tender to resist. I allow him to do what he wants. He's tentative, with each step waiting to see if he has permission to continue. Eventually, I get on top of him and slide him inside me. He seems shocked. I let myself enjoy the warmth of his flesh on my body, the pleasure of physical intimacy. I close my eyes until I can hear him climax. He falls asleep with a smile on his face.

The next morning Cyril wakes and gets ready for work. He showers, gets changed, and has some cereal. He comes back into the bedroom. My eyes are still closed, and I'm resisting getting out of bed. He kisses me on the cheek.

*Thank you.*

I hear him leave. It should sound strange, him thanking me for sex. But somehow it doesn't. Politeness and pragmatism may be the absence of passion, but they're not the absence of kindness or maybe even love. He's not unaware of the awkwardness of our "situation," and I'm glad of that. It's one less facade to maintain, one facade I don't have to sprinkle with details to create the illusion of authenticity.

I get up and shower too. I remember Cyril inside me. Like the running, sex has knocked me back into my body a little more, out of my head, out of my flickering, exhausting mind.

# forty-nine

David Aguilera has brought somebody with him. His name is Jasper Jones, like the artist, but this Jasper has likely never heard of the American artist from the fifties. And this Jasper is not keen on being here, mildly irritated at being pulled away from whatever he was doing. Painting? thinks Detective Rose playfully when she sees his mood.

Aguilera probably pressured the guy to come down to the station with him, more than likely overstated his position in law enforcement to do so.

*So what is it?* asks Detective Rose.

*I did some cross-referencing. The thing about this case—I'm kind of getting obsessed. I keep playing it over in my mind, and I've been looking at all the angles, and I think I've got something.*

He looks at them, hoping to get their attention. Lewis gives him an impassive look. Jones shifts irritably.

*Jasper, tell them what you saw.* Jones exhales like it's a chore.

*I was going to my shift at the hospital. I'm a pediatric nurse.*

*This is early morning on the fifth,* adds Aguilera.

Jones continues, *I pull out of my driveway, and this woman almost runs into my car.*

*A woman?* says Rose.

Aguilera is excited, as he sees the surprise on Rose's face.

*I got a look at her. She seemed—I don't know—like there was something wrong with her, and then she ran off.*

*Tell her about the blood,* Aguilera prompts eagerly.

*Oh yeah. It looked like she had blood on her knees, as if she had fallen or something.*

*The alley. She had fallen in the alley,* Aguilera can't wait to add.

*Did you see what she was wearing?* Lewis asks.

*A dress, maybe dark red or brown.*

Rose motions toward the envelope. Lewis pulls out the photo of Mary and hands it to Jones.

*Was this her?*

He takes a look and then nods casually. *Possibly?*

*Possibly?* Aguilera wants more.

*I mean, I think so. It was just a moment in the middle of the night, and then she ran off.*

*Take another look,* presses Aguilera, *and think hard if—*

*It's okay.* Rose steps in.

*His house is 1.6 miles from Mark Matthews's house. He leaves for the hospital at around two thirty a.m. You add the fall in the alley, maybe running with an injury; it matches,* Aguilera says, sure of himself.

*Thank you for coming in, Mr. Jones. We may have some more questions later if you don't mind, but for now, that'll be all.*

He grumbles something and leaves.

*Thanks, Jasper,* Aguilera calls out, and then he turns his attention back to Detective Rose.

*So who is she?* he asks eagerly. *It's got to be her, right? It has to.*

*A one-and-a-half-mile radius of downtown suburban houses and shops is a big area, Mr. Aguilera. How are you getting this information?*

His expression changes as he wonders if he's in trouble here.

*Ma'am, nothing but footwork and my connections with the neighborhood watch teams. I read the files, and I knocked on doors, with consent and at an appropriate time so as not to disturb people.*

*You're not misrepresenting yourself, are you?*

*No, ma'am.*

*It's an ongoing investigation, Mr. Aguilera. You have been helpful, but please remember the boundaries here.*

*Yes, ma'am.*

*Thank you. You can go now.*

He salutes her. It's over the top, but he's pumped, knows he's done a good job.

Rose and Lewis are left sitting in the reception area. Rose has gone silent again, letting the tide wash in. She stares into the middle distance for a long beat.

*Guess it's time we bring her in.*

# fifty

The hospital smells like bleach. My nose itches, and my skin feels brittle. A very old man with an oxygen tank sits in a wheelchair in the corridor. He's alone. His shoulders are hunched as he stares at the ground between his feet. He has tubes running out of his nose, and there's an IV drip in his arm. A thin gown covers his skinny thighs.

I walk into Joyce's room, but in her bed, there is a large Black man. His stomach is swollen like a grapefruit. He's watching *Judge Judy*. She's pointing her finger at a young guy in a cheap suit. *No, you don't talk. I'm talking now.*

Joyce has been discharged. Her health insurance has lapsed, and she can't pay. The receptionist is sorry, and she gives me her sad eyes. I feel the anxiety bird flapping around inside my rib cage as I try to find a bus route that will get me near her home.

How will she treat her diabetes? What about the dialysis she needs for her kidneys? Her blood pressure meds? Who will look after her? *Now that I've killed her son.*

I have to walk a mile after the bus drops me off. I feel as if I want to run, but I don't. My cheap black shoes with their fake leather cut into my ankles. It's painful to walk for a long period, and I want to take them off.

The neighborhood is run down, and there are many empty plots overgrown with weeds.

I find her place. It's a five-apartment complex of single-story units, all semidetached, with the parking bay in the front. There's an old Ford Mustang with a flat tire surrounded by leaves.

I knock on the door, but no one answers. She's probably in bed and can't get up that quickly, I think. The anxiety bird flaps louder in my chest. She shouldn't be alone. People need care: the old, the young, the heartbroken, the destitute, the angry. We all need people to cushion the blows, help soothe our fears.

The curtains are closed. It's dark inside, and I can just make out an empty sofa in the corner and a table in the kitchen area.

*Mrs. Matthews? It's me, Mary.*

Nothing. I walk around the side of the apartment. The grass is thick, and there's a tall, unruly bush against the side of the house. Black barbed seeds stick to my shirt and hair as I push past. The side window is open slightly, and a thin curtain sways gently in the breeze. I call through the window, *Mrs. Matthews?*

Craning my neck, I manage to see into the room through a small gap in the window. There's an unmade bed, but it's empty. There's a pile of medicines on the bedside table and two empty glasses and tissues. The bedside light is on.

*Mrs. Matthews, it's Mary, Mark's friend.*

And then I see it: a foot on the floor. At first, my mind doesn't make the connection. Why is there a foot on the floor sticking out from behind the bed? And then my brain catches up and screams: *That's a body! That's Joyce!* The bird goes manic in my chest.

*Joyce! Joyce!* I'm shouting, banging on the window.

I reach in, clawing at the latch, trying to open it. The bushes scratch my arms. I get the latch open. The window flies open and bashes against the wall, almost shattering the glass. I pull my body up onto the ledge, adrenaline giving me more strength that I normally have. *Thump!* I fall onto the carpet inside her bedroom. My head and my hip hit the ground hard. I crawl over to her. She's red in the face and wheezing. Her body is trembling. I don't know what to do. Joyce is bouncing about in spasms. I try to hold her down.

*Shu shu ga* . . . She's trying to say something. My panic is debilitating. I want to chide, curse, snap myself out of it. What is she saying? She's dying, dammit! I remember my phone, and so I start scratching in my bag, but my movements are too fast, too hasty. My phone falls out of my hand as I try to pull it out. I snatch it up again and dial 911.

*Shu shu ga*, Joyce is saying.

I try to punch in the number twice, getting it wrong the first time. Then somewhere in the pandemonium of my mind there's a small voice: *Sugar*, it says quietly.

*Sugar?* I ask Joyce. Her eyes widen with recognition. I run into the kitchen. My eyes dart around. It smells pungently of dirty dishes and old cat food. On the counter I see a jar. I rush to it, and my hands knock it over as I try to grab it. It's sugar. I take what's left in the jar and run back to Joyce.

The 911 operator is trying to get the address from me as I try to feed Joyce the sugar to balance her glucose levels. I read about that at the library one day. I read lots of books. I read self-help books for personal improvement; I read poetry for culture; I read encyclopedias for empirical knowledge; I read romance for what I thought were the ways of love. But where were the books on the crushing horror of day-to-day living? *How Not to Get Set Up for Murder*? Or *Eliminate the Terror of Life in Three Easy Step*s.

*Step 1: See step 2.*
*Step 2: Just kidding, there are no steps, just more hell and more terror. Ha ha ha.*

———

I watch the ambulance as it takes Joyce to the hospital. One of the neighbors has come out to watch the incident. He's sitting in a chair on his porch and has a soda in one hand like he's watching some form of entertainment. Once the ambulance has driven away, he pushes the chair back from the table and goes inside again.

Joyce will be back at home soon. She cannot afford to stay. They will stabilize her and then discharge her. She'll be alone in the house with no one to care for her, and this will happen again, I'm sure of it. Will she just die here? Does anybody care? The weight of these thoughts pushes down on my small shoulders. *You did this, Mary Williams,* the voice tells me. *You killed her son, the only person that could help her. This is on you.*

I clean her bedroom. I wash the sheets and hang them on the fence to dry. I sweep under the bed and under the couch. There is dust and dirt everywhere. I put her soiled clothes in the washer, and I try to restore some order in her closet. I clean the bathroom, the toilet. I clean dishes caked hard with old food. I clean the kitchen counters with bleach. I take out six bags of trash. On the outside, it looks like I am cleaning Joyce's low-rent apartment, but I know it's not really cleaning. It's penance for what I've done to her; it's the only thing I can do for her to keep myself from curling up in her black ringed bathtub and drowning in the quicksand of my guilt.

———

The bus drops me off, and as I walk the two blocks back to Cyril's apartment, I can't shake the feeling that Joyce Matthews is going to die. How can she not? There's no one to take care of her. She clearly has a chronic, life-threatening diabetic condition, and without the money for the treatment she needs, there's nothing to—

Emma!

Oh God! I forgot about Emma. I start running. My heart pounds. It occurs to me that this level of anxiety is unsustainable. Something is being permanently damaged inside me by this extreme stress. Will I too be rushed away in an ambulance with its sirens blaring? I was meant to collect Emma from her bus stop for an extra visit, and I forgot. She was supposed to come and study after school. *Please, God, let her be okay.*

As I turn the corner, I see she's not there—just the empty bus shelter. I look around, but there is no sign of her. My legs want to buckle under the weight of my compounded fear. Something is about to crack. I run home like I've never run before. I run up the stairs, three at a time. My lungs are burning and I'm sweating. I burst into the apartment.

Emma is there. She's playing chess with Jaya in the living room. The afternoon sun is streaming through the windows, flaring off the glass of orange juice on the table next to the chessboard. There's some Indian flute music playing from somewhere. Cyril is making pancakes. I hear the sound of a muffled cell phone vibrating.

They all look at me as I stand there. They seem confused as to why a person would look the way I do, with my wild eyes and scratches on my arms and face from the bushes at Joyce's apartment. I've lost my ability to modulate my emotions: too much fear that I have abandoned Em, too much gratitude seeing she's safe with Jaya and Cyril. My face does peculiar things. That muffled phone is still ringing somewhere. Someone is asking if I am okay. Jaya is looking at me with concern. Em, impatient, embarrassed, is imploring me, *Answer your phone.*

I realize it's my phone that's ringing. I reach into my bag, wanting to go outside, reenter, do this again, not be the crazy woman bursting into their calm, normal world. I find the phone. It's a number I don't recognize.

*Hello.*

*Hi there, is this Mary Williams?*

*Who is this?*

*This is Detective Rose with the Atlantic Beach Police Department.*

# fifty-one

My mind is a planet, vast and in turmoil. A planet at war: fear and shame and worthlessness and insanity, all fighting savagely for dominance. There's almost no part of this world that is not under attack in the full-blown pandemonium of this horrific battle. The land is scoured and burnt black, the air acidic and toxic, rubble and ash where there were once buildings and houses. But on some remote island, a small collection of hopefuls lives . . . busy tilling soil and planting seeds for a potential future where there is not just war and madness but maybe something else—something like hope.

On rare occasions, I visit that place and walk in the fields, my hands caressing the golden corn nourished by the warm sun. I imagine my daughter and Jaya and Cyril and me making this work, letting the light shine through our cracks, illuminating each other with kindness. An unconventional family, yes, but a family nonetheless, like in a quirky novel.

There have been moments with the three of them when I didn't see Jaya blackout drunk and too fragile to function in the world or Cyril with his desperate need and fundamental insecurity or Emma permanently damaged by her broken family and her poverty-stricken mother. I didn't see all this. The sharp edges had been worn down by the hopeful people of Hope Island. In those brief moments, I thought this could work; we were a gang of misfits adding color to Em's life, making her well rounded and wise.

Then my phone rang, and the policewoman said my name. And a bomb was dropped on the kind people of Hope Island, and limbs were blown off, the fields of golden wheat were decimated, and people ran screaming and burning.

It was the reality bomb, and no island of hope can survive that.

I hang up the phone, but I can't say anything. How can I? My life has been blown to smithereens. I want to drop to the floor. The reality train is plowing through the carefully constructed scaffolding that's been keeping me upright.

Cyril comes over. *Are you okay?*

There are no books yet written, no words yet invented, to describe my state.

Em is upset. She storms off to the bedroom, trying to hide her tears of embarrassment from Jaya.

Jaya looks at me. He knows.

He comes over. He moves slowly, the calm combat doctor who has sewn back together many shredded bodies and obliterated minds. But I can tell even he is shocked at the amount of suffering I'm clearly having to endure.

*Why don't you put the kettle on,* he asks Cyril. Cyril, ever grateful for his leadership, hurries off.

*It was the police,* I tell him in a voice I don't recognize. He tries to hide his concern.

*Text them back and tell them you will return their call shortly.*
I look at him, unable to move or think or live.

*It's okay. I'll do it. Give me your phone. Go talk to Em. Tell her you are fine, that you're just going through a lot of stress. Reassure her that everything is going to be fine.*

He looks at me. His eyes tell me to get moving, get stuff done, not surrender to the fright. He nods and takes my phone.

I nod back, trying to rally.

---

Emma is lying on the bed. She's angry and embarrassed. She needs her mother. I find a strain of calm. I explain to her that I will deal with my "situation" and that we're going to be okay. I just need a little time to get back on my feet financially, I tell her. I acknowledge that I'm not handling the stress very well and it's a difficult time for me. I apologize for my behavior. I explain to her that I have a friend who is really sick, who may die because she can't afford her medical treatment. I tell her I went to see her. I tell Em about finding Joyce on the floor. I try to explain that my agitated state is due to the stress of being unable to help my friend.

I sit on her bed, stroking her hair, trying to rationalize my behavior so she will understand. It works. She clings to these explanations like a drowning person clings to a passing raft. I know that these are well-intentioned lies designed to help her. But they are still lies. My world is headed for devastation, and I know that there's nothing I can do about it. But still, I made Em feel better. I did my job. I fought the good fight.

Em finishes her homework in the bedroom, still fragile and not wanting to face Jaya and Cyril. Am I losing her? Have I made it too hard for her to be with me, with the inferno of my life? Is David, even with his enraged frustrations, becoming the less stressful option?

I can't lose her. My anger rises. No, we used to be friends,

Em and me. It was always us. This is not right. I think of that man, that man who used me to do that terrible thing to his boyfriend.

There's a flutter deep in my gut, but this time I know it's not the anxious bird. It's something else, some new thought, a seed of a thought:

*He can't get away with this.*

A humble seedling. But I sense its roots sinking, slowly, deeper into my being, like it's going to be here for the long haul, like it's going to be around for a while, and it wants to grow strong and steady enough to withstand the hurricanes of doubt and the storms of insecurity. It wants to take me over eventually.

This is Mary the Strong.

And she wants more than anything to bear the fruit of vengeance.

# fifty-two

While the world laughed and mocked Donald Rumsfeld when he said there were *known knowns*—things we know we know—and there were also *known unknowns*, Detective Rose didn't laugh. She thought Mr. Rumsfeld had a clear insight into how to make sense of a complicated world. Because that's how she works. She is never bewildered by things she doesn't know. She just sees them as known unknowns. She knows, for instance, that she doesn't know exactly how Eric Wilson killed Mark Matthews to collect the insurance money. It's just a known unknown. This gives her a sense of peace because as a detective, her job is to make the unknown known. This isn't the problem that has her missing breakfast, something she rarely does. This isn't the problem that caused her to wake up at three thirty last night and remain restless, tossing and turning in a tangle of sheets, until she finally got out of bed at six.

The problem is Mary Williams.

Mary Williams's role in the murder is also a known unknown, but a cloud of *unknown* unknowns swirls around her, aspects of the crime Detective Rose doesn't even know she doesn't know about.

Detective Rose calls Officer Lewis into her office to discuss the case with him. She likes Officer Lewis in that he has no imagination. And sometimes, she needs that—just the facts.

*So what do you think? About him?* She gestures at the picture of Eric on the murder board.

Officer Lewis likes being called in for an opinion. He has never really been able to connect with his boss, and there is always the hope that in these rare, seemingly less guarded moments, she might reveal some detail about herself that will make her less of an enigma to him.

*I think without a murder weapon he's walking.*

She thinks that, too, but it helps to hear it from him. They've searched and searched with the quiet determination of a group of worker ants. There isn't an inch of that house that they have not turned over, dug up, cut into, x-rayed, unplastered. They've searched both Eric's apartment and Mark Matthews's house. They've combed through the trash, the surrounding area, the local dumpsters. They found some extraordinary things: two dead puppies in a briefcase, $1,000 cash in a plastic bag stuck in a hollowed branch of a large tree, and a pink dildo with the words *Florida for Trump* written on it.

But no gun.

*We're checking gun sales in the area and the online directory of the neighborhood, but it's a very wide net, so it's going to take us some time to wade through it all. And then of course there's the black market, so you know. This could all take a while.*

He purses his lips. *There are a lot of unknown unknowns here.*

He's not sure if he's using this in the right context, but he knows that she likes the saying, and he's trying to connect with her the best he can.

*Did the lab come back with results from the hand scrub?*

They tested Eric's hands for gunpowder residue and found

none. Rose got them to do it again, but they found nothing on the second test either. Then she made them test for any unusual cleaning aid other than soap. Maybe Eric Wilson had thought of this and had tried to clean off any residue with bleach or something. They found something, and they're now running a fourth test to try to isolate what the anomaly is.

But Officer Lewis knows that she is stabbing in the dark. It's probably just some unusual moisturizer or something. It's not as though everybody uses the same cleaning products to clean their hands. But Lewis has seen this before, his boss going down some seemingly obscure rabbit hole, indefatigable, digging and digging, finding nothing, getting pushback for the seemingly fruitless endeavors and their waste of resources, only to find something that cracks a case wide open. Like the time she had them test the stomach contents of a suspect's dog. They identified yellow lentils and tracked it down to a nearby Indian restaurant. The suspect had given his dog leftovers. The restaurant identified the suspect, proving he was lying about his whereabouts. It's that kind of no-stone-unturned grunt work that got her a reputation of being a great detective.

But she's stumped here, and Lewis can tell. He wants to say something encouraging. But then he thinks better of it, and the awkwardness sits between them in the office like a third person.

Mary Williams called back, and they got her to agree to come in at 2:00 p.m. But Rose is still not sure how to handle the interview, who should do it, or what angle they should take. Mary Williams is surrounded by unknown unknowns, and that makes Detective Rose nervous.

Lewis leaves, and Rose sits in silence again. The tide washing up, receding, the rhythms of providence revealing and concealing what they will.

# fifty-three

I want to tell the police everything. I have no capacity to lie. They will understand, surely, that I am not a murderer, that I was tricked by an evil man into killing his boyfriend. I want them to arrest him. I want to go to the trial, and I want to confront him on the stand with the truth, with details of the truth and the obviousness of the truth. I want to face the lying bully. I want to fight the good fight too. I want to be Arjuna, the warrior who, once aware of his righteous duty, picked up his discarded bow and went into battle to fight the good fight. I'm tired of being a doormat. I'm going to lose my daughter this way. I won't have it anymore. I'm ready to fight.

I tell all this to Jaya. Cyril has gone out. I can hear myself haranguing Jaya: *This is what I must do, and I must do it now.* My voice is strident and without nuance. I know that Jaya understands this. Is this not the teachings of the Bhagavad Gita? Is this not what he taught for so many years, to fight against our lower nature? And with Jaya by my side, I feel emboldened and ready—ready to speak my truth.

But Jaya disagrees.

He tells me to lie, to say what Eric instructed: that I was

helping to care for him with his migraines and that was the extent of our relationship. He says I should say as little as possible, and if I don't like the way it's going with the detective, I should tell them that I need to speak to my attorney. And he says that then I should get up and leave because that is my right. He says I must not be naive.

I want to slap his smug, experienced face. He doesn't know how fragile I am, how I want to protect even the slightest resilience that surfaces in me like a starving wolf protects a scrap of meat. I don't want to lie. I need to tell the truth, make people see who Eric Wilson really is. Jaya tells me to take deep breaths and calm down. *Calm down?* Does he not know that in the history of the world no upset woman has ever calmed down because some man has just told her to do so?

---

We drive to the police station in silence. He offered to drive me in his old Prius. I reluctantly agreed.

Sitting inside the windowless room with two chairs and a small rectangular table against the green wall, I shrink from the bold warrior woman carrying truth as her weapon. Now I'm just scared. I'm a little girl, and my father is shouting at the dog for puking on the carpet. He kicks the dog in its side. The dog yelps and skitters off with its tail between its legs. Now my mother is chastising him for his outburst, but he doesn't like her correcting him. (What man ever does?) He's shouting back, trying to maintain his rights, his dominion; they're both screaming. I hide under the bed, squeezing my ears shut, afraid of the big people and their loud voices and their lashing out.

I wait in the small room in the police station for about twenty minutes. There's a half-broken pencil on the floor under the desk and a wire wastepaper basket in the corner, which contains an empty Styrofoam cup with a brown-stained rim. These items seem forlorn in the bleak room.

I'm shrinking with each minute I wait. I can't lie. I can't tell the truth. What will become of me? When Detective Rose walks in, I stand and smile meekly.

She smiles in return. I was not expecting this: the kind face of a middle-aged woman.

*Thank you so much for coming in, Ms. Williams. I appreciate you helping us out.*

She explains about the murder. *As I'm sure you are aware*, she adds. She tells me they know I was helping Eric Wilson, the deceased's boyfriend, with his migraines.

She is in no way accusatory and speaks in a soft, steady voice.

Can she see how fragile I am? I wonder. Like one jab in a weak spot might shatter me into a million pieces of anxiety, clinking to the tiled floor.

*Can you tell us where you were that night?* she asks gently. But I know that this is a test. Eric told me what to say and what not to say.

*I was at the Mia Bo coffee shop. I don't sleep so well,* I add as a way of explaining being out at two in the morning. Detective Rose nods agreeably, but I know that there are other things coming that I won't be able to explain, other questions coming that I won't be able to answer.

*So far from home? There's a coffee shop only two blocks away from your apartment.*

Questions like that.

I smile at her and shrug. The lying tenses me up. Like each lie turns the key of a jack-in-the-box. Too many turns, and I'm going to explode. But for now, I just shrug.

I see her looking at me, trying to get a read on me.

Sometimes, you have to break smaller principles to uphold bigger principles, Jaya told me. Avoiding imprisonment is a bigger principle. Lying is the smaller one. I try to let that make me feel better, unwind a rotation on the windup key.

I exhale a little, release a fraction of the extraordinary tension trapped in my body. *You can do this, Mary*, I tell myself.

And then Detective Rose says:

*There was a woman spotted running away from where Mark Matthews was shot that night, just after the murder took place. We have a witness that identified a picture of you as that person.*

*KAABOOM!*

An atom bomb detonates inside my head.

Someone saw me!

The shock of this is unholy, destroying any semblance of composure I have. I can't control what my face is doing. How did I think I could just sit here and lie? To the police! My mind seizes; I'm dumb and mute; the aftershock of the blast pulses through me.

I stare at her.

Detective Rose seems concerned for me. I'm on my feet, clumsily knocking over the chair, trying to make my way to the door.

*Law, lawyer,* I manage to say as I stumble out of the room. My head is swirling. The corridor is full of other police officers. One of them is staring at me, his brow furrowed, trying to decipher the look on my face. I don't know how I'm walking. I'm screaming at myself in my head, *They know! They know!*

I bump into a mail cart. I push through the front doors. Outside now. The sun is too bright. I can't see. My foot misses a step. My hands grab at the railing. And here's Jaya now, at my side, taking my arm.

*I've got you.*

He leads me down the stairs to the Prius. I look back. Detective Rose is standing at the top of the stairs, watching me, studying me.

I get into the car. Close the door. Shell shocked. I turn to Jaya.

*Someone saw me.*

# fifty-four

Detective Rose stands at the top of the stairs watching as Mary Williams gets into a late-model red Prius and drives off. She stands there for some time, replaying what just transpired but exercising her observer mind, letting the details bubble up and surface on their own.

There is still information, subtle information that needs to surface. But for now, there's one thing Rose does know for certain, one thing that she didn't know twenty minutes ago, and that is that Mary Williams is undeniably involved, somehow, in the murder of Mark Matthews.

But this information doesn't bring clarity. It brings the opposite: gray, a fog. She has followed rules her entire life. If you take one and then find another one and put them together, you will have two. It's not complicated. If there was a guilty person and you found the evidence of their guilt, they would go to jail. And then came Nicky Valdez. A guilty person didn't go to jail. Even though he was guilty and even though they had the evidence of that guilt. One plus one didn't equal two anymore. And that made her deeply uncomfortable. Like she had to learn a new math if she was to understand the world.

She should arrest Mary Williams. She has enough for that, at least, and Rose knows this woman would crack under a more severe interrogation. That's what she would normally do: add the ones and then get the total she requires. But something is telling her to wait. Something is telling her this might be new math. She needs to look in the gray.

It hurts her head to think like this. Like looking too hard at her son's cubist painting. But she also knows that the comfort of routine, how she has always done things, is a false refuge. It doesn't take into account the Nicky Valdezes of the world. And not considering the gray is a mistake she is not prepared to make anymore. Detective Rose knows she is not the most dynamic person on the force, nor the most intuitive, nor the most intelligent, but she does know this: she learns her lessons and seldom ever makes the same mistake twice. And if Mary Williams is involved, she sure as hell is not going to get away with it.

She wants to stay out there longer, stay out on the steps overlooking the parking lot, and let her mind float around the incident with Mary Williams and her stumble out of the station. But the sun on her face is getting too hot now, and she's conscious that maybe they're watching from inside the station. She turns and heads back inside, her head full of gray.

---

Lewis is pacing around her office when she arrives. It's distracting, and she wants to ask him to leave, but she doesn't say anything. She's trying to be a more tolerant person. *Be more personable,* she was once told during a job evaluation.

*You've got to get a warrant. She's hiding something for sure. She's in on it, a hundred percent. Did you see her face? She thought she could just lie her way through this. Do you want me to speak to the judge to get the warrant? Judge Simmons can help. I can go now.*

Rose knows this feeling, this enthusiasm, but she's an old-timer. She also knows its dangers. Too much clarity means no gray. No gray means you're missing something. Detective Rose can see that Lewis is getting irritated at her pause, her hesitation. He thinks this is a no-brainer, but everything is a brainer, even the no-brainers.

*You saw her—she's about to break. We charge her with murder, and she, along with whatever lawyer she can afford, they'll spill in an instant to get a reduced sentence. We've got this, Detective. I'm sure of it. We need to get her phone records, bring the lab over to her place.*

But Rose won't be rushed. She needs to think on this. Something is bothering her. She can't shake the feeling. She had this with Nicky Valdez. But she was unable to articulate it, and she had no evidence to corroborate the feeling that things were not as they seemed. She ignored her gut, and Nicky Valdez walked. She rushed to get a verdict, and he walked. She won't be rushed again. But she also knows the force has a low tolerance for hunches that don't align with the evidence. Sooner rather than later, she'd better find something washed up on the shore, something big, like a murder weapon, if she wants to do new math.

# fifty-five

*I can't go to jail. I have to tell her the truth. It's the only way. They know I'm lying; someone saw me.* SOMEONE SAW ME! I'm shouting, nearly hysterical.

*You told me to lie! You did this!* I'm lashing out. Jaya is driving in silence, not defending himself.

*I'm not going to jail. What about Emma? I can't go to jail. I can't. I can't.*

I'm slowing down now, after ranting like a maniac for a good ten minutes in the car. It's exhausting, and the fear behind the rage is seeping out too, making me small and vulnerable.

*What should I do?* I plead like a child. Jaya looks at me. He understands, I know, but he says nothing.

*Tell me. Tell me! God dammit, help me! You can't just say nothing. They're going to put me in jail. What will happen to me if I tell her the truth? Will I still go to jail?*

I hate this desperation. I hate the pleading. I hate being so weak and passive and needing Jaya to lead the way. I hate that I know no other way. I hate that this is what got me here.

The rage rushes back. I'm punching Jaya as he drives.

*Why? Why did this happen to me?*

He's pulling over into a parking lot overlooking the beach. I'm pummeling him with all I've got, everything boiling over.

*What's going to happen to me? Why did you tell me to lie? Why? Why?*

But I can't keep this up and break down crying. Jaya holds me as I convulse in his arms. We stay like that for a long time. I'm broken by the intensity of my suffering. The tears don't stop. My body shudders.

———

The sun starts to set. A light onshore wind pushes the surface of the sea into patchy smudges of foam. A seagull hovers in the wind, staying in a spot just above the railing, hovering without flapping its wings. I slowly climb up from my pit of despair. I exhume myself from Jaya's arms, sit back in my seat, and look out at the water. My face is hot, and the tears have wet my cheeks and the corners of my eyes. I've depleted my emotions and now can only stare out into the harsh reality of a destroyed life. The car is silent. Jaya looks into the middle distance, no stranger to staring at the remains of a once-whole life.

Eventually, *What must I do?* I say in a different voice.

We sit, watching the ocean, the great wide sea, the keeper of secrets. Maybe it knows the answers.

The question hangs in the air between us.

*This is not the time for grace and kindness,* Jaya tells me.

I don't know what that means. I see a seagull with one leg hopping onto the railing, chasing another bird away from a lone breadcrumb.

*You have to lie more.*

# fifty-six

*He's leaving the country, on vacation.*
*But he can't. He's under investigation.*
*We don't have anything to hold him on. You know that.*
*But . . .*
Officer Lewis closes his eyes, exasperated. Detective Rose feels the same way. She's just a little more experienced in dealing with these situations. Her outrage trigger has worn down over the years.
*We've got to arrest Mary Williams, now, before he goes. If he goes, he's gone. She has information on him for sure. Did you know that his insurance paid out?*
*I know.*
*So?*
She looks up at Officer Lewis. She knows she's going to have to act. She's going to have to act without the time she needs to walk along the shore of her mind and see what has washed up. She won't have the opportunity to turn over the objects in her hands, blow the salty sand from their crevices, and see if these things fit into the puzzle or are to be thrown back into the vast, secret sea. She knows this is when mistakes are made,

when there's not enough time to consider the ramifications of any course of action, when the danger of not making a decision can be as severe as the danger of making the wrong one.

*We can't wait. We have to arrest her.*

Rose understands she has no choice.

*Okay.*

Lewis's eyes widen; she knows he can't believe he's actually gotten through to her.

*But I need a day.*

*He's got a flight on—*

*I need a day. And then you can go and arrest Mary Williams.*

She gets up, swipes a file from her desk, and leaves.

# fifty-seven

The baby is crying. She has him on her hip, bouncing him while trying to talk to me.

*I was away in Kansas. I didn't know. I thought she was in the hospital. What happened?*

We're standing in Joyce's kitchen. Joyce is asleep in the other room. I'm sure the baby's crying is going to wake her.

*She couldn't pay anymore, so they discharged her and sent her home. She ran out of medication. I came around to see how she was doing . . . and she . . .I saw . . . I called 911, but once they got her stable, they discharged her again.*

She starts crying. *I can't—I can't pay. I don't have any more money. My kids, the day care—just for the two days a week—it's too much.*

Shanna Lovett is Joyce's neighbor. I remember her from the funeral. She was pushing Joyce in the wheelchair.

*What's going to happen to her?* She's scared. I don't know what to tell her. *If she can't get her medication, she's going to die She has diabetes. It's severe. My father-in-law died of that. The kidneys—she needs that medication. Why can't the state pay? They can't just leave her to die.*

I know all this. But I don't know what to tell her.

*Her son, Mark, he used to pay for her, and then...* She shakes her head. *I tried to help. I can't bear to see her suffer like this.*

*It's okay. I'm sure we can . . .* I don't know what I'm saying, but I have to say something. *I'm sure something will work out.*

*I have a list of what she needs.* She's fishing around in her bag. The baby is still crying. He's red in the face and looks furious. She takes out a crumpled piece of paper, points to the list.

*Here. These two are the most important. This one, this is for sleep, but these other two, she has to have these every day.*

Shanna hands me the list.

*Thank you. I tried to help,* she says. *It's just—she was kind to me. When my husband left, she would take the baby sometimes. She used to bake cookies for us.*

Tears smudge her eyeliner and roll over her cheeks.

*We live just two apartments down, if you need anything.*

The baby is still fussing. He won't settle. She transfers him to the other hip.

*I have to go and feed him.* She touches my arm. *Thank you. You're saving her life.*

She leaves through the back door. The screen whacks against the doorframe, leaving me alone in the kitchen, feeling like an impostor.

How can I save Joyce? Shanna has mistaken me for a normal person. It's almost comical that she thinks I am able to effect positive change in Joyce's life. She doesn't know that I'm the one who caused this.

I move into Joyce's room and stand in front of her bed. Eyes closed, she wheezes through her mouth. She looks weak and pale. I'm still. The house is quiet now that the crying baby has gone, no sound but the slow inhale and exhale of her frail lungs.

Is she going to die alone in this bedroom?

Joyce starts to cough. Her watery eyes flutter open. I come over and help her sit up. I bring a glass of water to her lips. She sips weakly. The water spills down her chin, onto the sheets. She feels for her medicine bottles at the side table, knocking a few onto the floor as she does so. How will she do this all alone?

*I've got this. It's okay.* I gently shake a single pill into her unsteady palm. I notice the pill bottle is two-thirds empty. It takes a few tries for her to swallow the pill, but eventually she gets it down. I open the curtain a little to let some of the afternoon sun into the dark room.

*I signed the papers,* I tell her. *I'll take them to the hospital today.*

Joyce needed someone to be her medical power of attorney. There was no one else. She asked if I could do it. What could I say? Tell her I would be of no use to her, as I'd probably be in jail shortly for the murder of her son?

She looks at me. A strange expression comes over her face.

*Am I . . . going to . . . die?*

I look at her. I need to lie.

*If you go, will I . . . will I die?*

*(Lie to her, dammit.)*

The breeze ruffles the thin curtain. She looks at me, afraid. I hear Jaya's voice in my head: *You need to lie more.*

I come over to her side of the bed. Take her hand and look her in the eyes.

*Everything is going to be okay.*

# fifty-eight

Detective Rose has called to say that they're going to arrest me for the murder of Mark Matthews. She explains that it is a courtesy call. She wants to give me the opportunity to surrender myself at the police station so that they won't have to send officers to come and get me. Her tone is soft and understanding. She mentions that she is aware that I have a young daughter and that she will be handling this with as much discretion as possible.

I hang up and walk into Jaya's room in a daze. I tell him what has happened like it is happening to someone else, emotionless and near disembodied. He tells me to say nothing. He says that he will get his lawyer to bail me out. He says that he will take Em to see Cyril's play and make some excuse about my absence. He takes me by both my arms, and he tells me that I have the right to a fair and just life, and that if the world won't give me the courtesy of that, then it is up to me to create that life for myself. He tells me that the only way to do this is to resist the pressure that the police will put on me to confess. I have to stand up for my right not to be cheated. I have to stop allowing people to push me around. He tells me that he can help me, but I have to respect myself enough to help myself first. I try to listen as he is speaking. It is hard because the insecurity monsters are marauding around in my head, stomping loud, ready to revolt, demanding attention before they burn the place to the ground.

*If you tell the truth of what happened, you are confessing to murder. Please understand that, Mary. Do not say a thing. All you have is your word that Eric told you that this was an assisted suicide. He will of course deny that. Don't. Say. Anything.*

I'm sitting in the passenger seat as Jaya drives me to the police station again. I'm struggling to concentrate. My eyes see people traveling in cars in front of us, the blue sky, the passing shopfronts, but my brain can't compute any of this above the noise of the screaming in my head.

We arrive at the police station. This is not a dream. It's not a novel. It's real. It's my reality. I have to get out and face my reality. I have to face the most terrible thing that can happen to someone.

Jaya looks at me. *A lawyer is coming. Say nothing until he gets here.*

———

There's a loud, angry woman in the reception area arguing with an officer behind the desk. I don't hear the words. I just hear her fear masquerading as rage. The officer isn't concerned, and he goes about shuffling papers on the desk behind the countertop. The woman has a little boy standing next to her. He stands in front of the counter, but he's too short to see over it. I'm led past him in handcuffs. They are cold and hard against my wrists. The little boy sees me. He looks afraid. For me? For the people I've done something to?

They lead me into the interrogation room, and I sit down

on a chair. My hands are behind my back. I know this room. I was here before. How long will I be able to survive this before I break down in tears and confess?

Detective Rose walks in with an officer. She smiles compassionately. I feel the warmth of coming tears. I grit my teeth. I don't want her to be kind. If she's kind, even if I know she's trying to manipulate me, I will break down.

*I'm sorry we had to bring you in like this.*

(*Don't cry, don't cry. She's going to put you in jail, and you will never see Em again.*)

*Hopefully, we can get this over with as soon as possible. I'm sure that you can help us and get back to your life sooner rather than later.*

Back to my life? They're not going to put me in jail? I look at Officer Lewis. He looks angry, irritated at Detective Rose and the way she's dealing with me. He wants to hurt me. I can see it in his narrowed eyes. I look back at Detective Rose.

*We wanted to get a better sense of your movements on that early Monday morning, things you may not have told us before.*

*Someone saw me*, a voice screams inside my head.

The detective looks at me, signaling that it's my time to talk. I look at the officer and his pinched face.

*I need to . . . speak with a lawyer . . . before we start. Then I can . . . speak . . . with you.*

I struggle to put the sentences together.

*I understand that, of course, and that's your right, but this is the easier way. We have some loose ends that you can tie up for us; then we won't have to charge you, and you'll be free to go. If we charge you, we have to put you in a jail cell, and it may not be so easy for you. By the book means you go to jail now. I don't want you to go to jail, Mary.*

I look at her, and I can feel my chin trembling. The outside is holding, but the inside is collapsing. The scaffolding is crumbling, the walls are disintegrating, and the support poles are falling over.

She looks at me. She's trying to connect.

*I don't believe you killed Mark Matthews, but you have to tell us who did.*

I can see Officer Lewis is shocked by what she has just said, but it's hard for me to understand things because I'm holding on to a log. I'm in a raging river about to get swept away; the current is strong, pulling hard at my legs and body. My grip on the log loosens. With great force, the current is pushing me to tell this kind and understanding woman what really happened. I hold on, my knuckles whitening.

*If you help me, I can help you.*

She's like a caring mother talking to her child.

Is she really kind? Can she help me? I need help. I need someone to be kind.

The water is rushing around me like a thick wet hand around my body, trying to dislodge my grip from the log.

*Tell us about Eric Wilson.*

I look into her eyes. I see a person that looks like she cares. I can tell her. I can tell her about what Eric Wilson made me do, how he lied to me. She will understand. She will help me. How many times must she have seen women being exploited by men like this?

*I am your chance here, Mary, a chance to actually help you, possibly your only real chance that you don't end up in jail for the rest of your life.*

A hand slips off the log. Only one hand is left, keeping me from dropping into the raging current, tumbling down the river of truth.

They know he did it. If they know, why are they asking me? Why aren't they arresting him?

My mind is flipping out. I purse my lips, trying to keep my emotions in check. He did it. I must tell them he did it, tell them he didn't pull the trigger, but he might as well have. She will understand.

I slowly shake my head. *No.*

Detective Rose notices my distress. She knows I don't have much resistance left.

*He's not the kind of person that you should protect, Mary.*

She's right. He's a monster. Why am I protecting a monster? Why does he get away with this? How could he ruin my life like that? How could nothing happen to him after he tricked me into doing such a thing? My fingers start to slip off the log; I feel them going, the relentless, powerful current pulling hard at my legs. My fingers are sliding over the slippery bark of the log. I say nothing, but my mind is screaming, roaring, TELL HER!

I can see that Officer Lewis disapproves of me, of my lie. I can see Detective Rose's disappointment growing too, her sadness about the kind of person I'm choosing to be, the person that chooses to lie.

*He's getting on an airplane tomorrow, and without any evidence, we can't stop him. He's getting away, Mary.*

I can't take it anymore.

I open my mouth . . . I have to tell her. She will help. She'll understand it wasn't my fault.

*What did he do with the gun, Mary? Tell us, please.*

I feel myself slipping, slipping off into the river, unable to resist. I try to hold on, but I know it's over. Her voice is soft and kind. I have to tell her. I can't lie anymore. *I'm sorry, Jaya, but I'm not like you.*

I let go of the log.

I open my mouth to confess, and as I do—

*Stop lying to us!*

The pinch-faced officer is speaking now. His eyes are hard, and his voice is angry. It's jarring.

Suddenly the atmosphere in the room changes.

*We know you were dropped off by an Uber just before two, close to Mark Matthews's house. Twenty minutes later, you were running away from his house covered in blood. You knocked into a trash can and almost ran straight into the reversing car of Jasper Jones. We have witnesses. Stop lying to us.*

He fires these statements at me like sharp slaps to my face.

Detective Rose is looking at Officer Lewis. Her face has changed too. Her jaw is tight and her eyes narrow. She's not angry at me but at him. I'm confused. Why is she looking at him like that?

Everything is suddenly different in this little room. My hand reaches back up to grab the log.

Maybe I can't trust these people. Maybe I'm making another mistake.

There's a knock at the door.

It opens, and all the tension rushes out of the room like a hot wind.

*Her lawyer is here.*

I feel relief surge through me, the voices in my head momentarily muted. I sit there, my shoulders slumped, exhausted by this near drowning.

Detective Rose gets to her feet, her lips pursed and her jaw set. She looks at Officer Lewis.

A tall skinny man in a suit appears and says to Detective Rose, *We posted bail.*

He turns to me. *Hi, Mary. We can go.*

For a moment, I don't know how to move, frozen to the chair. Then my brain reengages, and I get to my feet.

# fifty-nine

Detective Rose knows Lewis is getting the brunt of all the cumulative years of her frustration with the force, the sloppy courts, the injustices, the bureaucracy, a life that has never quite reached the level of satisfaction she hoped for despite all her efforts to do the right thing.

She also knows that his mistake, although clearly the reason why Mary Williams was able to resist confessing before her lawyer came, is nonetheless understandable, coming from a rookie police officer who is still inexperienced in the art of interrogations.

Still, she can't stop herself. She shouts with a toxicity she has never shown to anyone before. She chastises him for his teenage impudence, his embarrassing naivete, his arrogance, his stupidity. She says things designed to hurt him. She wants to cause him pain.

He drops his head and takes it, and then he leaves, and she is left sitting in her office, fuming.

The residue of her anger hangs in the air like a sticky mist. She knows that people heard her outburst, and she is embarrassed by her lack of self-control, but more than that, she's upset at how she made Officer Lewis feel. Who goes out of their way to make someone feel so horrible about themselves? She doesn't like that side of her. She has never wanted to behave like that, but something that used to be a vague blurry shape has now come into very clear focus.

She knows that her time as a police detective is over.

She knows she has to resign. She won't let this job turn her into a horrible person.

She calls him in later and apologizes. She actually wants to cry. She hasn't experienced that kind of emotional state since her father died. Officer Lewis can see how contrite she is, but she knows he isn't sure how to respond, having only ever seen her as stoic and composed.

He asks her what they should do now. She tells him that they're probably going to trial. Mary Williams will be unable to survive a trial. But it won't matter because Eric Wilson will end up somewhere in the Bahamas, enjoying cocktails on the beach.

She says these words with a detachment that seems to unnerve Officer Lewis, like a valuable part of her has gone, and now she's just a lost ghost wandering around the room.

*We have to do something.*

She shrugs. *You have any suggestions?*

But Officer Lewis has nothing, lost without his mentor's leadership, just a rudderless boat puttering aimlessly around the lake of *now what?*

# sixty

*You'll need to tell him what actually happened that night*, Jaya tells me. He explains attorney-client privilege and how I'm not incriminating myself by telling the truth now. *He needs to know so he can formulate your defense.*

We're inside a Waffle House. There is a mom tapping on her phone in the next booth. Her two kids are pouring maple syrup over their pancakes. They seem happy to be out.

Jeremy, my lawyer now, is Jaya's old college friend. He does *pro bono* work, but he's mostly retired. He's tall and skinny, a fidgety beanpole, moving around in his seat, crossing and uncrossing his legs. He says that without a murder weapon, they still might have enough to convict me with the eyewitnesses and the contact with Eric, a love-triangle motive.

*That's absurd. He's gay*, says Jaya. Jaya is intense, more intense than I've seen him before. His sleepy ease has transformed into a potent focus. It's like he's fighting for his own freedom.

*No, he's bisexual. He had a girlfriend in high school*, says Jeremy.

*You know that?*

*No, but that angle is not gonna be hard to establish if needed.*

I barely listen. I can only think of one thing: he got away with it.

That man took me for a fool, a pathetic and desperate woman who he could manipulate, and he was right. Mary the Strong rumbles inside me.

Jeremy chews the inside of his cheek when he thinks. His leg bounces. He's like a lanky teenager who needs a run. He's pressing me about evidence inside the house. Did I touch something? Leave any prints?

*If they find evidence of you in the house . . .*

He doesn't finish, but I know what he means.

*Mary?*

I turn to Jaya. He's looking at me, concerned. *Are you okay?*

I nod. But I'm checking out. Something is happening inside of me; I can feel the energy in my cells changing, charging.

Jeremy wants to meet again on Monday. We agree on a time and a place. When Jeremy leaves, I tell Jaya I can't afford a lawyer.

*He'll do it pro bono. Don't worry about that.*

We drive back in silence, Jaya at the wheel.

———

I'm standing in the bathroom. My feet are rooted to the ground. My arms hang by my sides and feel heavy. I don't know how long I have been standing like this. There is a roaring inside my head. Like the sound of a waterfall. It's white noise, loud and echoey.

The sound is constant. This is Mary the Strong starting to roar. The volume is still muted by decades of oppression and abuse, but I hear her.

I hear her.

The shower is running. I don't recall turning it on. Hot water is hitting the curtain. I stand there. I'm about to step into the shower when I realize I'm still wearing all my clothes.

I turn it off. My hand burns from the scalding-hot water as I reach inside the curtain, but I don't really feel it. I look at my red wrist. I feel nothing. My mind is preoccupied with this roar of the once-dormant me.

I hear talking now. It's Jaya. He's talking to someone. He is using his telephone voice.

*You coming tonight?*

What is happening tonight? There is a world out there that I have no awareness of.

*I'm sorry to hear that. I'll tell her you called. Bye, Em.*

Emma!

Hearing her name is like an injection of adrenaline. My eyes widen. My soul slams back into my body. My hand suddenly hurts from the burn. I can feel my heartbeat in my chest. I look around, move over to the sink, and wash my face.

I walk into the living room.

*Em called. She said she's not coming tonight.*

Jaya can see the confused look on my face.

*You know,* The Things We Do*?*

Still nothing.

*Cyril's play.*

Then I get it. It's Cyril's big night. We were all going to watch him.

I call Emma. I can tell instantly, even with the roaring in my head, that something is wrong.

*What is it?*

She knows I know. She knows I won't stop asking until she tells me. So she does.

*Dad.*

I feel the blood heating in my veins. My eyes narrow like a lizard's.

*What?*

She's silent on the other end of the line. I feel a rage growing inside. I want to grab her and shake her and scream TELL ME. I know what he has done to me over the years. I will not allow him to do this to her.

*He shouted at me. It's nothing. He said sorry. It's just . . . I don't want to go out. I'll see you tomorrow.*

She wants to blow this off, but she's upset. She's normally safe with him. His anger at me never transferred over to Emma. Somehow, she was spared his rage. But now that's changed. I can't let her take this.

*You have to tell him, Emma.* I use her full name. *You have to tell him that this is unacceptable, that you won't tolerate him shouting at you like that. You must, Emma; this is important. It's straight abuse, violence. This is your life, and it's about how you deal with the world. This isn't something you just blow off. This kind of thing . . . you can't let it happen.*

She's retreating. I can tell. But I'm insistent. She has to understand this! I keep going. She retreats further. She doesn't want to hear this, but she must. This is her life. This is how she agrees to let the world treat her.

*You can't let him get away with this, Emma.*

And then she cracks.

YOU DID! *All those years of him shouting at you, breaking things, hitting walls, and you didn't once say anything! You let him get away with it. Leave me alone! Stop trying to live your life through me. Just fucking leave me alone!*

She hangs up.

I'm shocked. She's never spoken to me like that before.

# sixty-one

I sit with Jaya in the small community theater, watching a play about a passionate man who kills himself to prove his love for an indifferent woman. The set designers have painted a backdrop of the apartment windows and the city lights outside. There is a couch and some other props. The lighting team up in the rafters follows Harold, the lead actor, as he emotes and strides around the living room. I sit there like a normal person, not someone about to be convicted of murder. The play is too long or too short; I don't know. All I can do is concentrate on one thing. One sentence that loops around in my head.

*You let him get away with it.*

There is nowhere to hide from those seven words. There is no hole deep enough that can shield me from the illuminating truth of that sentence.

*You let him get away with it.*

I did. It's true. Not once did I ever tell him to stop. *Stop shouting in my face like that. Stop abusing me with the volume of your anger. Stop punching the wall near my head. Stop taking the frustrations of your life out on me.*

Not once.

I'm stunned by this reality. Not only because of what I allowed to happen to me for all those years but also because of where that has led me now. I let a man get away with tricking me into killing someone. He's about to walk free, and I'm about to go to jail for murder.

He's getting away with it.

I envisage Detective Rose with me in the interrogation room, her eyes imploring me to see the reality of that.

———

The spotlight up in the rafters slides onto Harold, standing on the stage and shouting up at the heavens, declaring his undying love for the unmoved Olivia. The light creeps over the heads of the audience until it lands on me. It's me! I did it. I allowed this to happen. I let him get away with it. I am the star of this show. I sit there cringing under the light of this realization.

Emma is on the stage now, standing there, looking down on me, telling me, *I appreciate what you want me to become, Mom, but I never saw any examples of that. I was never shown how to be strong or at least to respect myself enough to ask someone to stop doing something that harmed me. I only had you as an example, and you never said anything. You took it, like you felt you deserved it.*

I'm sweating, exposed under the spotlight. The humiliation of truth. Maybe that should be what I call my own play.

———

The play comes to an end. I remember almost nothing about it, except the intense man with the mustache, Harold. He was left dying on the floor with a knife wound to the gut. Cyril came on and said his lines at some point. I hope that he was okay, that people liked him. He's just like all of us, bewildered and flawed, trying to be happy as he dreams of being a great actor.

The clapping at the end of the play knocks me back to the present moment. The actors all bow. Cyril catches my eye. He's beaming and happy. I try to smile back.

We're mingling in the foyer after the show, chatting with the actors. Everything seems normal, but it's not. I feel like I'm standing there naked, like everyone can see that I let Eric get away with it.

Harold comes over to our little island of Jaya, Cyril, and me, and he immediately takes over the conversation. All our attention shifts to him. Jaya congratulates him on a riveting performance. Harold hands me his business card. *For all your acting needs,* he says, with a flamboyant flourish. I look at him like I'm stoned, two steps behind, trying to keep up with the witty banter.

It's hard to concentrate. Jaya looks at me every now and again. He knows the life I once led is over. There is only the question of what will happen now, what will survive—if anything—after the devastating consequences of my actions have played out. He knows there's enough to fell me. Just standing upright, with Harold gesticulating next to me and Cyril laughing at his weak joke, takes everything I have.

*I let it happen.* There is no one to blame but myself. I am the architect of this life I lead. I failed. I'm going to jail. *I let this happen.*

———

I'm sitting on the edge of the bed, staring into the middle distance in the dark room. Cyril has gone out to a bar with the rest of the cast and friends. He didn't push me to come. I had no energy to resist or to go. Jaya stepped in and took me home. I wonder if I will ever be able to look Emma in the eyes again. She knew what was happening all along. I didn't stand up for myself, and now she will know that another man has done the same thing to me. And again, I didn't stand up for myself.

And now I'm going to jail for murder.

I sit in the dark.

I sit for a long, long time.

The darkness sits with me, like a friend. The stillness sits there too. I don't want to move.

Darkness.

Stillness.

Truth.

And then, from the black, I feel her resume control. Mary the Strong. But she's come now not to save the little Native American boy from the school bully, not to protect Emma from the abuse of her father. She's come for me.

Deep inside I know, as I have always known, I must act . . . for me. I have to fight the good fight . . . for me.

Sometimes you have to reach the bottom before you can go up.

I know there is only one way forward now.

I am Mary the Strong. Hear me roar.

I look at the business card in my hand. *Harold Macintyre— Thespian for hire. For all your dramatic needs.*

# sixty-two

For some reason, I'm not wearing shoes. I feel the cold and wet sand under my feet. It's dark out, just the moonlight reflecting off the sea. There are no waves, only a gentle lapping on the shore. I try to get my bearings, looking at the beachfront houses and trying to remember. I see the porch and its missing wooden slat, and I walk from the wet shore over to the dry sand. The dune grass whips my ankles as I climb over a small mound of sand, toward the porch of the house. I walk up to the porch, drop to my knees. They sink into the sand, which is still warm from the day's sun.

I start digging with my hands in the place where I dug after that fateful night. I dig slowly and methodically. I am Buddha in a growing hurricane. I dig with the weight of thirty-nine years, eight months, and twenty-seven days behind me. I know what this is. This is fate. This is the pull of destiny.

And then the ring on my finger clicks against something metallic.

It's ironic. He's already shown me how to do this. He's taken me through a dry run. He's made me comfortable with a gun in my hand. He's made me comfortable with its power. But it's not the irony that is making this a real problem for him.

It's my rage.

I am Mary the Strong.

While people like him and David often use their rage so unconsciously that it eventually becomes dull and ineffectual, that is not true with me. My rage is new and hyperfocused. Where their rage made them less, mine makes me more. This is the suppressed rage of a thousand slights. This is the cumulative rage of a generation.

And as I'm shoving the gun in his face, I can see his shock is not because I've got a gun. His greater shock is seeing my ferocity.

I'm not the Mary Williams he knew before. Frankly I'm just as surprised as he is. Who knew I could pick up the bow and fight?

But then sitting on that bed, in the dark, I began to feel this building wave, this strong pull of fate. I may have let him get away with it at first, but some bigger force, some increasing rage, was sure as hell not going to let it happen anymore. That wave carried me here, into his room, with a gun pointed at his once-smug face.

# sixty-three

Eric has thought of many things. He has planned for many outcomes. But what he didn't realize was that if you take away everything from somebody, they have nothing left to lose, and a person with nothing left to lose can be very dangerous.

*Get up.*

The gun barrel with the silencer is inches from his face.

*What—what the fuck are you doing?* He's protesting, but he's getting out of bed, arms in the air.

*Go to the kitchen.*

Eric Wilson is fully awake now.

*Go!*

It shocks him to hear her, this new voice, this new person. Hands in the air, his eyes on her, he backs into the kitchen.

There's a piece of paper on the counter with Joyce Matthews's bank account number written on it.

*Transfer Mark's insurance money to where it rightly belongs.*

Eric Wilson knows that he won't do this. It's just not possible. He's been through too much to get the measly $685,000 (after taxes and the extra legal fees he had to spend to get the damn thing expedited). He's not going to give one cent of it to the sick old hag who's just about dead anyway.

Maybe he can charge Mary, catch her off guard. He's stronger than she is. If he can knock her to the ground, he can overpower her. He's got to be careful, though. If a stray shot goes off . . . that could be tricky. Maybe he can call her bluff. There's no way she's pulling that trigger. He knows he needs to buy some time, try to get a better read on whatever the hell has gotten into her.

*Do it!* she spits through clenched teeth.

It's a bit much, thinks Eric, this new badass woman, like an overacted version of Uma Thurman in the *Kill Bill scene* where she takes down the Deadly Viper Assassination Squad.

He takes his phone and starts opening his banking app. She's got the gun on him. He notices the tremor in her arm. She's scared, he thinks. She can't follow through with this. He's moving slowly, deliberately making mistakes opening the app, using the drop-down menus, punching in the code. She keeps looking around, like someone might see her. The longer this goes on, Eric surmises, the more the wind is going to leave her sails. He knows he's dealing with a weak woman who's not going to be able to maintain this false bravado for very long.

*Hurry up!* she yells at him.

That's more convincing, thinks Eric, but still, he can see through it. He puts the phone down on the kitchen counter and looks at her.

*You're not going to shoot me,* he tells her calmly.

*Don't try me,* she spits out.

*You know I'm not going to just give away what's rightfully mine.* She balls her hand into a fist. *Don't push me over the edge.*

He smirks, knowing that she's overplayed this. She needed a more nuanced performance, more Natalie Portman, less JLo.

There's a noise at the open back door. Someone's there: a man complaining about the disturbance, saying that they need to keep it down or he's going to call the police. But now he stops midsentence, seeing the gun in Mary Williams's hands. The color is draining from his face, his mouth falling open. Mary is grabbing him and pushing him inside, onto the floor. He's begging for his life, babbling.

*Oh God, oh God. Please, no.*

Mary raises the gun, pointing it back at Eric.

*Do you think I'm fucking playing around here?* Her face is enraged. Eric takes a step away, as if the ferocity of her voice has knocked him backward.

YOU THINK I'M FUCKING PLAYING AROUND?

She swings the gun toward the man lying on the kitchen floor.

PHHHHT

She shoots him in the gut.

Eric's eyes widen. He makes a noise in his throat, choking back shock.

She swings the gun back at Eric.

*Transfer the money. Now!*

Eric is stunned. He sees the blood spreading through the man's white shirt like a blooming crimson rose.

He realizes she is no longer sane. She's lost her mind. Her whole being is flooded with rage. The gun is shaking in her hands.

*Okay, okay.*

Eric is panicking now, suddenly petrified of this crazy woman. His fingers struggle as they try to punch in the account number. He's nearly in tears. Mary is inhaling and exhaling next to him like a wild boar.

*Do you think you can just do this to people and get away with it? You had someone killed, and now his mother is dying! You piece of shit!* She's shaking, whispering this like a curse as he tries to focus on typing in the right numbers.

*I'm sorry, I'm sorry. Please don't shoot me. Please, please . . . There, it's done, it's done.* He shows her the screen. She picks up the paper and checks the numbers. He puts the phone down on the counter.

*You deserve to die.* She puts the gun to his head. He cowers.

*Please! I beg you, please!*

*Do you think I'm weak? You're weak! You're the weak one.*

She takes his hands and wraps them around the gun and points at her own head. *Go on, do it. Pull the trigger! You worthless piece of shit. Go on!*

But Eric is broken, too scared to do anything in the face of such crazy rage. He drops to his knees.

*I thought so.*

She looks at him blubbering at her feet, a broken mess.

# sixty-four

Detective Rose is dreaming when the phone rings. It's a dream where there's a bad guy hiding in the garage and she's trying to tell the officers to go and get him, but there's no sound coming from her mouth. No matter how hard she tries to shout, no one can hear anything. They just talk among themselves, unaware of the approaching danger. She's had many versions of this dream: being stuck in a hole with people walking on the path above, but no sound coming out when she screams for help; being trapped in a locked room and the people in the next room not hearing her cries. She's even had a dream where Nicky Valdez is robbing a 7-Eleven with her partner inside, but he can't hear her yelling at him to arrest him, and Valdez walks out of the store with all its cash.

She often wonders what it might mean. She even googled it once: *why can't my shouting be heard in dreams?* The prevailing theory, according to dream science (although she thinks that's a pretty liberal use of the word *science*), was that she was not being heard in real life. She thought about that for a few minutes but concluded that she didn't feel that frustration.

*Hello.* She answers the phone, groggy.

*Eric Wilson is hiding the gun he used to kill Mark Matthews in a pot under his sink. His prints are all over the weapon.* It's a man's voice she doesn't recognize, and before she can fully comprehend what she's just heard, the caller hangs up.

---

The streetlights streak over the windshield while I drive Jaya's Prius back to the house. Harold is sitting in the passenger seat. He's got his shirt hiked up, and he's cleaning the fake blood from his stomach and removing the sticky tape that held the blood pouch in its place.

*I'm sorry you had to ruin a good shirt.*

*All great art requires some suffering.* He smiles.

He looks at me. It's a look I'm not accustomed to, something like respect.

*That was pretty impressive back there*, he says as he removes his wig. *You should act; that was convincing.*

I take a moment to realize he thinks it was a performance. A car drives past me with the windows open. Teenagers are singing in the back seat.

*There's no going back now, baby.*

---

They find Eric Wilson cowering in his closet, where Mary told him to stay. They find the gun in the pot under the sink. He's mumbling and frantic, desperate to explain. *She killed him, both of them.* He takes them to the living room, but there's nobody there. He's got his hands cuffed behind his back. He is struggling, demanding his lawyer, shouting that he's been set up. *She did it! She did it! That crazy bitch. She's the one.*

Detective Rose coolly watches him from across the room as he stomps his feet like a petulant child.

*There was blood, all over. She must've cleaned it up. Do the scan thing on the floor with the light.* He saw that in *Gone Girl*. *You'll see. She killed him. She's crazy. She's a crazy psycho bitch.*

*Get him out of here,* Rose tells Officer Lewis.

*What? You're not listening to me!*

Lewis pulls hard on his arm, the cuffs biting into his wrists.

*Argh, that hurts!*

He swings his anger back to Detective Rose. He hates her. The worst kind of person. An ugly, dull, emotionless drone. He's outraged.

*I'll sue you for false arrest. I'll fucking sue you and the entire police force. I'm an eyewitness; I'm telling you what happened. You can't just ignore what I'm saying. Hey, hey, you . . . I'm talking to you. She was here!*

Detective Rose is ignoring him, acting preoccupied with something else. She knows how much this is getting to him.

*Hey, fucking bitch! You can't just—*

*Doefff*

Officer Lewis bashes Eric's head deliberately on the roof of the patrol car as he shoves him into the back seat and slams the door shut. Eric is bucking and raging now, his muffled threats as inconsequential as his feeble kicks at the back of the passenger seat.

Detective Rose looks around. But she's not surveying the external environment. She is sifting through the internal one. *What just happened here?* she wonders. The gun with his prints washed up on the shore . . . like a gift.

Lewis walks back, smiling smugly. *We got the bastard.*

# sixty-five

Detective Rose doesn't have any blue left, and there's a portion of the sea she hasn't gotten to yet. The store closes at five, and by the look of the sun on the horizon, that was some time ago. She could go into town the next day and get some more. But she wants to carry on painting. She's not half-bad at this. Who knew? She loves more than anything the feeling of being immersed in the scene, when her mind stops doing calculations and evaluations and another part of her takes over, the immersive part, the art part. Hours can go by like this, and nothing makes her happier.

She decides that the sunset over the surface of the sea tonight is just too beautiful to stop even if she has no blue left.

She dips her brush into the magenta oil and starts to paint the ripples on the ocean. A magenta ocean? She can't help but smile, wondering what on earth has become of her. Her son would be proud.

Part of her knows what happened to her. She remembers the day clearly. Sitting in the courtroom as Mary Williams lied to the judge, to the defense attorney, and to everyone else and said that she had seen Eric Wilson coming out of Mark Matthews's house at around two on the morning in question and that she saw that he had a gun in his hand, and she started running away in fear when he came toward her. Then she apologized to the police for lying previously, explaining that she had been afraid he would kill her if she said anything to anyone.

It was astounding to watch how this once-timid, once-broken woman sat there with such grace and inner strength and lied with such conviction. With her testimony and the life insurance motive and, crucially, the murder weapon with his prints on it, Eric Wilson was found guilty of the murder of his lover, Mark Matthews.

What caused Mary Williams to change? How did she learn to lie like that, a lie that ensured justice was done? Sitting there in the courtroom watching this all unfold, Rose was sure Mary Williams would be destroyed under cross-examination and the whole case would collapse. And when it didn't, it stunned Detective Rose into the realization that she had to go back to church, because clearly there were things beyond the comprehension of humans at play in the world. Some kind of providence was guiding all actions.

The result of that day in the courtroom was justice. A bad person was punished. A good person did something right, and evil did not triumph. But the abstract and contradictory method was enough to change Detective Rose for good.

She realized that for many years she had not trusted the system. She'd believed it was up to her to ensure that justice would prevail, because if she didn't do anything, it wouldn't. It was on her. That responsibility was so burdensome that she had been unable to live, unable to find joy, weighed down by the heavy duty of it all.

But sitting there that day, seeing Mary Williams, seeing the change in her, Rose realized that it was time for her to resign from the police force. She was not in control of the justice of the world. She had done her part, however small, and now it was time to retire, to take up watercolors and spend more time with her son.

She mixed the magenta with some yellow, making a rust color for the sun's reflection on the water. She felt happy. These colors made no sense, and that was perfectly fine.

# PART III

*To understand just one life, you have to swallow the world.*
   —Salman Rushdie, *Midnight's Children*

# sixty-six

A YEAR LATER

Jaya is nervous. They've been working together for months to get to this point. It's strange to see him like this, a pumped-up cornerman, giving his fighter a pep talk between rounds.

*He can only attack. That's his only strategy, blind aggression, trying to get you to panic. He's going to move quickly, sacrifice pieces to break open your defense. You're going to look vulnerable in places you should never look vulnerable.*

He takes her by her little shoulders, looks at her with his baby-blue eyes.

*But you're not. It's a smoke screen for the fact that he has no defense himself. He's trying to get you to panic. All you have to do is slow down. When he pushes the clock after thinking only for a few seconds and then making a brilliant move, slow down; think longer; push him off his game. Don't let him rush you. Don't go to him. Make him come to you. Be defiantly slow. Resist every instinct to match his pace and aggression. You'll see. Be patient, and he'll fall apart. He wins in ten minutes or he's done. I have watched his games. I've seen his history. Hold your own, Warrior Emma, hold your own.*

She's nervous, I can see. She's never made it this far. This is huge. This is the national championship finals. Her highest finish before this was a quarterfinal loss. Now she could win the whole damn thing.

We watch from the front row. They are playing on a stage that we look up at. The moves are projected onto the screen behind them. The boy starts just like Jaya said he would: super aggressive, sacrificing his bishop to get two pawns and completely opening up her king's defense. It's devastating. Someone in the crowd even gasps.

I don't care if she loses. I love her. She's a bright and brave girl for whom I will do anything. But Jaya's nerves are infectious, and I feel my blood start to pump a little faster as I notice his bouncing left leg. Cyril squeezes my hand when Em gets the boy's knight, but he doesn't really know what's going on. The boy then takes her other bishop and another pawn.

Just like Jaya said, the boy moves at a lightning pace. Move, hit the clock; move, hit the clock; move, hit the clock. It's like he's going to wrap this up in three minutes unless Emma can protect herself.

And then Emma makes a mistake. Moving her rook without any protection. People mumble. She looks shocked. She panicked.

He smirks. He looks at his girlfriend sitting next to his parents in the front row and gives her a wink. He takes Emma's rook. Jaya closes his eyes. She's done for. Em moves her bishop to take his king pawn, putting him in check. He smiles. He knows he can just take the unprotected bishop too. It's easy pickings; she's falling apart.

And then he sees it.

And then everybody sees it.

By moving her bishop, she's exposed the rook hiding behind

it, which now has a direct path to take his queen. And he can't move his queen; he has to get out of check first.

He's going to lose his queen. He swallows, his world of cheap pride and teenager swagger collapsing beneath him. It's over. She just needs to take the queen and play the game out, slowly and patiently grinding out her advantage to the end.

His eyes narrow. He's angry. She just beat him at his own game.

Jaya is squeezing and wringing his hands. He can barely contain himself. Cyril is wide eyed and happy, even though he doesn't know the game well enough to realize just how brilliant her move was.

I can see the boy wants to hurt her now. He wants to flip over the table, lash out, blame her. She looks back at him. Holds her look. Holds her own. It's an eternity. Someone has to give. Normally, this would kill me, but it doesn't now. I inhale it, accepting whatever comes.

And then the boy stands. He knows he's lost. He turns over his king, resigned. People are applauding. Jaya's running up onto the stage, grabbing Em in his arms, swinging her around. He's shocked, laughing. It worked. She won. She goddamn won!

Cyril is beaming. I'm surprised by the crowd's joy, by my little girl winning. I'm surprised by this sensation in my heart. What is it? Is this happiness?

———

The sun streams through the bay window, leaving a long, bright-yellow rectangle of light on the carpet. Checkmate, Em's cat, lies asleep in the center of the patch of light. Her tail flicks every now and again as if gently reminding her that at some stage, she should probably wake up and think about doing something with her life.

I walk out to the small garden out back to plant flowers. Diamond flowers. I wanted to grow them from seeds, but Cyril jokes that I have to start a wildfire first. Jaya and Em have taken to calling me Inferno. I wanted to make the new house nice, a sanctuary for us. I repainted, tore up the paving in the back, put in bay windows. I know I'm exhausting myself. I know I have to loosen my grip on this desire to make everything okay.

*Chill, Mom*, Em keeps telling me. I'm trying to do that, curbing my attempts to control a crazy world. I'm trying to sit in it as it is, not as I hope it will be.

Joyce Matthews died some time ago. She had no family left after Mark was killed. It turned out some pieces of paper she asked me to sign in the hospital a few months before put me in her will. In a bizarre twist of fate, that meant I inherited the money that Eric Wilson transferred into her account before he was arrested.

*Guilt,* I answered when Detective Rose asked me why I thought he had transferred the money to her. *For killing her son,* I added.

I used the money to buy this house, with its little garden and a magnolia tree that stands proudly at the gate, protecting us who live inside. The neighbor saw me working outside this morning. He said the magnolia tree is dropping its flowers on his lawn. He said I must chop the tree down. I thought about that—not the chopping down of the tree but the flowers falling onto his lawn. How nice, the pretty white blooms sprinkled over the green.

*I'm sorry, but I can't do that,* I told him.

The branches weren't hanging over his fence. It was just the wind that was blowing the flowers onto his garden. And who can stop the wind?

We stood there in silence for a moment. He stared at me

incredulously, this timid woman telling him no. He was looking at me, and I was looking back. I meant no threat. I didn't intend to challenge him or his right to a happy life. It's just, well, you see . . . I also have a right to be happy, and so does the magnolia tree, and sometimes you have to fight the good fight.

Sometimes you just have to hold your own.

Author photo © David Bloomer

## M. M. DEWIL

lived as a monk in North India for several years before moving to Hollywood to write and direct feature films. He now lives in Alachua, Florida, with his wife and two boys. *The Helper* is his first novel.